KATE'S TURN

A Tail of Two Kitties

This book belongs to

Kelly R. Kalisa

Other Apple Paperbacks
you will enjoy:

Afternoon of the Elves
by Janet Taylor Lisle

Turning Thirteen
by Susan Beth Pfeffer

Kool Ada
by Sheila Solomon Klass

E, My Name Is Emily
by Norma Fox Mazer

Dear Mom, in Ohio for a Year
by Cynthia Stowe

The Daffodils
by Christi Killien

KATE'S TURN

Jeanne Betancourt

AN
APPLE
PAPERBACK

SCHOLASTIC INC.
New York Toronto London Auckland Sydney

Thank you to Rosemary O'Brien, my high school ballet teacher, and to Thea Little, Melora Hardin, and the many other dancers who have shared their stories with me.

For their editorial assistance I am grateful to Lee Minoff, Teri Granger Martin, Nola Thacker, and Jean Feiwel.

ISBN 0-590-43104-8

Copyright © 1992 by Jeanne Betancourt.
All rights reserved. Published by Scholastic Inc.
APPLE PAPERBACKS is a registered trademark of Scholastic Inc.

12 11 10 9 8 7 6 5 4 3 2 1   7   2 3 4 5 6 7/9

Printed in the U.S.A.   40

This story was written for Melissa Lee Shankman and Emily Maverick Shankman of Eugene, Oregon.

One

Carole and I are sitting next to one another on the top bunk in my bedroom. Our legs dangle over the side. The bottom bunk is overflowing with the clothes I still have to pack before I leave in the morning.

"Look at the difference in our legs," Carole says. "Anyone can tell you're the dancer."

I look down at my legs. Even relaxed, the curves of my calves bulge. And my feet are automatically in turn-out. My right foot points east toward a poster of my favorite ballerina — Patricia Gordon. My left foot points west to the mirror over my bureau. Carole's normal legs and feet swing straight up and down — north and south.

"I got you a present," Carole says, reaching into her knapsack. She hands me a box that's wrapped in bright pink-and-silver-striped paper. "You're so lucky," she says. "We're only thirteen years old, and it's like you have a career already."

"I'll have to work hard going to regular school," I tell her, "plus taking three dance classes a day. Dance, dance, dance."

I shake the box. I'm sure it's stationery.

"But you love to dance, and you'll be in New York City," Carole says. "The kids in that regular school aren't regular at all. They're movie stars and TV stars and models. They're all like grown-ups already, making a living and everything. I'll bet they even pay you when you have a part in a ballet. And you'll take the subway and go to rock concerts."

I open the box of stationery. In the left-hand corner of each page, Carole has drawn and colored in a little pair of pink toe shoes with their pink ribbons curving down the left side of the page, creating a margin. "Carole," I tell her, "this is so pretty. I love it. Thank you."

"Look at the envelopes."

I flip to the bottom of the box and start laughing. Twenty-five envelopes all stamped and addressed to:

Carole Logan
Box 1069
Eugene, Oregon 97405

"I wish you were coming with me," I say.

"Me, too. Or that you were staying here. Who will I talk to? It's like you're leaving forever." Carole's freckled nose crinkles up as she tries to hold back the tears collecting around her gray-blue eyes.

"Don't cry. Please. Look, I have a present for you, too." I pull her present from under the pillow where I'd hidden it. I drop it on her lap and start to laugh.

"What's so funny?" She gives a tug to one of her light brown curls — the way she does when she's annoyed. "You're leaving," she says. "I'm crying, and you're laughing? It's not funny at all."

"Just open the present," I say, suppressing a giggle. She rips the paper off the gift and opens the box of stationery that I've made for her.

"Look how much we're alike," she laughs when she sees the paper. "We made each other the same present."

Because Carole loves art, I drew a tube of paint in the left-hand corner of each page. A stream of Magic Marker color starts at the mouth of the tube and flows down the left-hand side of

3

the page to create the margin. Every page has a different color. "It would look a lot better if you drew it," I tell her.

"No," she says. "This is great."

"Look at the envelopes."

She flips through the box and holds one up. All the envelopes are addressed to me.

Kate Conway
c/o Ruth Danner
156 W. 74th St.
New York, New York 10023

We both laugh until we're crying, really crying. Even though I'm sad about leaving my family and my best friend, that night I dream that I'm dancing around my room — leaping, turning, jumping until I fly right out the window and through the night sky. My body's not straight out like Superman's, but dancing all the way across the country — from Eugene, Oregon, to New York, New York — until I land on the stage at Lincoln Center.

At 8:30 the next morning, my father's yelling from the driveway, "Let's get this show on the road." My seven-year-old brother, Tommy, and my five-year-old sister, Judy, are already waiting in the car, probably driving my father crazy.

My mother's still sitting at the kitchen table, dabbing at tears. "It seems so unnatural," she tells me, "to send a child off at such a young age. Except for vacations, you may never live at home again. You'll live in apartments with other dancers. You'll be part of the dance company, and they'll be your family. You'll have a whole life we won't share."

I know that what she's saying is true. I remind her, "You said it was okay for me to go. You're the one who took me to all those dancing lessons. Besides, you have Tommy and Judy at home. They won't move away when they're thirteen. They don't even *like* dancing."

My mother gets up from the table and leans over to hug me. "Just know this, my little ballerina, you can always come home. What you're doing is difficult. A lot of girls don't make it. There's no shame in that." Now she's smiling.

"Mom, it sounds like you're hoping I won't make it as a ballerina so I'll come home."

"That's not true." She stands up and takes off her apron. "I want you to do what you want. And you want to be a dancer. I'm very proud of you. We all are. You've got the talent." She rubs her hands over my long, thin, muscular arms. "You've also got the body, and you seem to have the determination."

"What I don't have is time, Mom," I say,

looking at the kitchen clock. "If we don't leave right now, I'm going to miss my plane."

Our car horn makes two sharp *toots*. Then two more. Tommy and Judy are taking turns.

I throw my dance bag over my shoulder, and my mother grabs her pocketbook. We rush out through the kitchen door.

"Good-bye, house," I whisper as I close the door behind me.

"We'll be landing in about fifteen minutes, folks. The weather in New York City is sunny and sixty-five degrees." I push the button to bring my seat into the upright position, and check that my seat belt is fastened. I feel as nervous as I do before a performance. What if I don't like the other girls? What if I'm not good enough in the classes? I picture myself in Mrs. O'Brien's weekday classes in Eugene, and in Mr. Randolph's Saturday classes in Portland — always the star, the dancer who shows the others what to do. "Watch Kate. Do it like Kate." I wonder how good I'll be when I'm dancing with the best of the best from all over the country.

I rub my hair with my hands to check that every strand of dark brown hair is pulled back and securely tucked into my dancer's bun. I reach under the seat and pull my black dance bag a little closer. When I get off the plane I want to look like a dancer, turn-out and all.

Half an hour later I walk through the entrance doors into the airport receiving area. Someone calls out, "There she is." I look in the direction of the voice. A curly red-haired boy — taller than me, but looking about my age — stands next to a small, beautiful woman who's holding up a handprinted sign: "Kate Conway." I wave and move through the crowd toward them.

"I told you it was her," I hear the boy tell the woman. "I can always tell."

The woman ignores the boy and smiles at me. "Welcome, Kate. I'm Ruth Danner, your housemother." We shake hands as I say hello. The boy and I say hello to one another. I wonder, is he a dancer, too? I thought we'd be six scholarship girls living in Ruth Danner's house. No one said anything about boys.

"I'm Jason Danner," he says. "I knew right away you were a dancer."

"We have another plane to meet," Mrs. Danner tells me. "In international. She's arriving from Russia, and her plane lands in a few minutes. We'll deal with picking up your luggage later, Kate."

"Just think," Jason says as we follow Ruth Danner along what seems like miles of corridors, "Russia. It's the first time they've had a student from there. You'd think she was from outer space, my mother's so excited. I'll bet she can't even dance that good. Wouldn't that be a riot?" Jason looks straight at me, waiting for an answer.

"No," I say. "It would be awful for her."

"Yeah, but it'd still be funny. Everyone so excited, and then she can't even do a *coupé* without falling over."

So he knows what a *coupé* is, I think. Maybe he *is* a dancer. "Have you met any of the other girls in the house?" I ask.

"Everyone's there but you and this Russian girl, Olga Rominsky. Her name's written on the back of the card we held up for you."

"Maybe that's a sign she and I will be friends," I say.

He winces. "I get it. A sign that's a sign. Pretty corny."

"I didn't mean it to be a joke," I say.

I already know that Jason Danner isn't going to be one of my friends.

That evening we sit down to dinner around a big oval wooden table. Jason's acting like a real know-it-all. You can tell he loves the idea of living in a house with girls who've never lived in New York City before. "You have to be real careful on the subway," he tells us. "Last week there was a mugging right at the 72nd Street station. In broad daylight."

8

The doorbell rings. "That's quite enough, Jason," Ruth tells her son as she gets up to answer the door. "Saki is here. Remember, girls, he's the head of the company and the school. He's the master. This will be a very proper meal, with no giggling. And, Jason, behave. Sit up straight."

While Ruth is gone, Beth Randal, who sits next to me and is from California, asks Jason, "What if you don't have any money and they mug you, what do you do?"

"Always carry money. Or give them your watch."

"Lay off, Jason." It's Samantha Bellows. She's from Boston, so she's used to big cities. "You're trying to scare everyone for no good reason."

"Mug?" Olga asks. "What does 'mug' mean?"

Samantha puts one hand over Olga's and says, "Olga, mug is like rob." Then she puts her other hand over Beth's and says, "Just stick with me, girls. I can take care of anybody who's foolish enough to mess with me."

I envy Samantha's self-confidence. Earlier, when we were all talking about how scared we were that we wouldn't be good enough in dance classes or that we'd be injured and have to go home, Samantha said, "You give it your best shot. If it doesn't work out, you go on and do something else."

9

I wonder if Samantha will make it. I decide that the first time we go to watch the senior ballet company, I'll count how many of the ballerinas are African-American. I'd be real angry if Sam didn't get to be a professional ballet dancer because she has dark skin.

When Saki enters the room, everyone but Jason stands. I've seen Saki's picture in all the dance magazines, so I recognize the bald head and trim gray beard. In real life he's shorter than I thought he'd be, but he carries himself like a dancer, and even though he's older than my grandfather, he still has a dancer's body.

"Young ladies, Jason, good evening. Please, sit."

Ruth rings the little silver bell next to her plate to signal the cook to bring out our dinner. Saki and Ruth sit, and Saki looks around at us. "Now, each of the new young ladies, please introduce yourselves to me."

My empty stomach starts rumbling with nervousness. I'd rather dance for strangers than speak to them.

"We will start with our young dancer from my motherland," Saki says.

Olga stands, shakes her long blonde hair off her face, and looks Saki right in the eye. I wonder if her stomach is rumbling, too. "I'm Olga

Rominsky. I've come to America to study ballet, like I did in Russia."

"Your English is very good," Saki says.

"My dancing is good, too. I studied for many years, and I won a competition to come to America."

"Good for you," Samantha calls out. "ALL RIGHT!"

Everyone else is silent, wondering how Saki will react to Olga's outspoken self-confidence and Samantha's outburst. Even Jason is quiet.

"Well, there is much for you to learn here, too," Saki tells Olga. "I saw the video of your performance. We've invited you here to teach you."

"I understand," Olga says. "There is much to learn. A dancer always studies."

"Yes," Saki agrees. He nods to Beth. "Next."

Beth stands. She's the tiniest of us all — but strong and wiry. Her dark eyes are the same shade of brown as her long straight hair. "My name is Beth Randal, sir. From California. Thank you for the scholarship. It's a great opportunity for me to study at the National Ballet School." She's looking at her plate and sounding as though she's reading from a prepared speech. "I'll do my best, sir. I love to dance."

"Yes," Saki says. "Many girls love to dance,

Miss Randal. Unfortunately, it takes more than desire."

Ruth nods solemnly in agreement. I wonder if she ever studied with Saki. I've looked at all of the autographed photos of ballet dancers around the house and none of them is of Ruth. Yet she looks like a dancer, walks like a dancer, and definitely loves the ballet. I decide that even though Jason's an obnoxious twirp, I'll ask him about his mother the first chance I get.

Samantha stands. "I'm Samantha Bellows. Everyone calls me Sam. I come from Boston. You saw me perform in *Summertime*. That was a jazz ballet, but I want to be a classical ballet dancer. I know it'll be hard work. I think we all do."

"Good," says Saki.

My turn. I stand. I order my stomach to stop rumbling, take a deep breath, and say, "I'm Kate Conway from Oregon. I'm a dancer." Then I sit down.

Saki smiles at me and gives out a little laugh. "Very well," he says.

By now Alice, the woman who will come each evening to cook our dinner, has put big platters of spaghetti, salad, and Italian bread on the table. No one reaches for the food. We're all waiting for Ruth to give permission. Jason says, "So can we eat or what?"

His mother silences him with a stern glance. Saki looks at the two girls who haven't introduced themselves. "So let's see who remains," he says. "Oh, yes. Ginny Lee and Lyrice Crosby. Lovely young ballerinas both, am I correct?"

Ginny and Lyrice are second-year scholarship students and are a year older than the rest of us. They smile at Saki adoringly. I thought I looked like a dancer until I saw Ginny and Lyrice. Their bodies are tighter than mine, more supple. They hold their heads higher. Both have long hair pulled tight into dancers' buns, and pretty faces with delicate features. I can't wait to see them dance. I can't wait until I'm the one who's gone through a year of training with the National Ballet School. I can't wait until Saki smiles at me and says, "Kate Conway, lovely ballerina."

After dinner Ruth tells us, "To bed, girls. You've all traveled today and need rest. Dance classes begin tomorrow. We get up at 6:45 A.M."

I push my chair away from the table and take another look at the room we're in. It has the highest ceilings I've ever seen in a house. Heavy sliding wood doors separate the living room and dining room. A built-in floor-to-ceiling mirror, framed in the carved dark woodwork, is centered on one wall. It's a little distracting because, from my place at the table, I can see myself eating.

We climb the stairs to the second floor where the ceilings are still pretty high. There are three bedrooms on this floor. Lyrice and Ginny share the big front room. In the back Ruth has a normal-sized room, and Jason a smaller one.

Beth, Samantha, Olga, and I continue up to the top floor. There the ceilings are low and slanted, like an attic. Beth and Samantha share the front bedroom. Olga and I share the one in the back. There's a bathroom between the two rooms. Even though we've only been there a few hours, everyone already calls this floor "the new girls' floor."

"It's like we have our own apartment," Samantha says excitedly when we reach our floor. "In my neighborhood, a whole family lives on each floor of a brownstone. You know, separate apartments with a kitchen and everything."

"We don't have buildings this old in Eugene," I say. "I've never even been in a brownstone before."

"Why is this house named 'brownstone'?" Olga asks me as she and I go into our room.

"I guess because the stone it's made out of is colored brown," I tell her.

"Oh," she says. "I understand." She looks at her watch. "But I'm tired. In Moscow it is already daytime tomorrow. I can't think in English anymore. Good night, Kate." She starts to get ready for bed.

It feels strange to end the day without reading a bedtime story to Judy, or getting good-night kisses from my mother and father.

I go down the hall to Beth and Sam's room to hang out for a while and talk some more. I hear them giggling and talking on the other side of their closed door. They already sound like friends. I'm too shy to go into the middle of that, so I go back to my own room. I miss Carole and think I'll write her a letter to tell her what's happened so far, but suddenly I'm too tired. I look at Olga. She's already asleep. I wonder if we'll be friends.

As I'm getting ready for bed, I remind myself that I'm in New York City to become a dancer, not to make friends. I lie in bed wondering what class will be like, worried that it was all a big mistake, that I'm not good enough to study with the National Ballet School, and that Saki will realize they made a mistake the first time he sees me dance with the others. I hear someone coming up the stairs and see the silhouette of either Ginny or Lyrice in the hall, going into our bathroom. I hear her throwing up her dinner. I guess I'm not the only one who's nervous.

15

Two

The next morning the six of us are in the dressing room with nineteen other girls who will be in all of our dance classes. Everyone is putting on identical dance clothes — black leotards over pink tights. I wish I could wear my gray plastic warm-up pants and tie an old cut-up sweatshirt around my waist the way I did at home, the way I've seen Patricia Gordon dressed for class and rehearsals in *Dance Magazine*. "I don't know what I'll do when I see Patricia Gordon in real life," I tell Beth. "Do you think I should ask her for an autograph?"

Ginny, who's dressing right behind me, says, "Kate, you can forget about autographs. We

16

barely *see* the senior company. They take class and rehearse upstairs. If we see them at all it's on the elevator, and then they're all gabbing to one another and swinging their dance bags in our faces. It's like we're not there." Ginny looks at the big clock over the lockers as she leaves the dressing room for the studio. "Don't be late," she calls to Beth and me. "Madame Rostov hates tardiness."

Ginny seems totally calm, so I decide that Lyrice was the one who threw up last night. What I wonder is why she didn't use her own bathroom.

When I walk into Studio Three, with its long mirrored walls, most of the students are already lined up in places along the *barre*. An elderly man, sitting at the piano in the far corner, is putting his sheet music in order. I take a place at the *barre* between Ginny and Sam.

Madame Rostov comes in, and we all stand straighter. Even though she's a little stocky, I can tell she's a dancer. It's not just because she's wearing a long nylon dance skirt over a black leotard, or that her dyed hair is fixed in a dancer's bun. I can tell because she carries herself like a ballet dancer.

"Hand on the *barre*. Arm out. First position." We all do it. She nods to the piano player and says, "*Plié*." Class has begun.

An hour and a half later we're back in the

dressing room. My leotard and tights are drenched in sweat. I have never in my whole life taken such a hard class.

"It's the same class as in Russia," Olga says. Sweat trickles down her face into the dimples near her mouth. "It was a good class, yes?"

"Yes," Ginny agrees.

"Wasn't the combination wonderful?" Sam says. "I bet the *corps de ballet* does the same one."

Beth is sitting on the long green bench in front of the lockers, rubbing her knee. As I wipe my wet neck and shoulders with a towel, I go over to her and ask, "Did you hurt yourself?"

"It'll be all right," she answers, not looking up. "It pops sometimes. I'll put ice on it when we go back to the house."

"That won't be until dinnertime," I remind her. "And we have our two other dance classes, one of them on *pointe*."

She looks up at me. Her eyes say she's in pain, but she tells me, "Look, Kate, it's nothing. Don't make such a big deal about it, okay?"

Lyrice comes into the dressing room dancing the combination we learned in class and humming the phrase of music that accompanied it. She was clearly the best dancer in the class, with Madame Rostov commenting on the progress Lyrice had made over the summer, and how well she'd maintained her slim dancer's figure. Everyone in the dressing room is watching her out of the corner of their eye as they pretend to be paying attention to something else, and they're all probably thinking what I'm thinking: I wish I could be that good.

"Anybody got something to eat?" Lyrice asks. "I'm starving."

Ginny hands her the container of milk she got from the pay machine. "You can finish this."

"Never mind," Lyrice says. "I'll just have water."

At lunchtime, Lyrice and Ginny go to a Greek diner with girls they knew from last year. Beth, Olga, Sam, and I go to a pizza place across the street from the ballet school. Olga looks excitedly around at the booths and tables packed with lunchtime customers. "In ballet school in Moscow," she tells us, "we always eat in the school cafeteria. We don't go to a restaurant for lunch." She pats her pocketbook. "I like to have this scholarship lunch money."

"Me, too," I agree.

"Let's celebrate our first day of classes by splitting a deluxe pie," Sam suggests.

"I'm for that," I say. "Pizza is my favorite food. And I get so hungry when I dance, I could eat a horse."

"Ugh!" Olga says with a look of total disgust.

"We don't eat horse in Russia."

"It's just an expression," I tell her, and try to explain what I meant.

Later, as we're dropping our paper plates and cups into the big orange plastic garbage can, Sam comments, "We've still got a half hour until our next class."

"What should we do?" Beth asks.

"Let's go to the ballet bookstore," I suggest, "and get posters to hang up in our rooms. I bet we get a discount because we're students."

"You're on," Sam agrees. "But first, let's go over to Al's Jazz dance studio and pick up a schedule. I took classes there when I visited my aunt last summer."

"A schedule?" Beth asks. "You're going to take jazz classes? I thought we're only allowed . . ."

"Just once in a while," Sam explains. "On a day off. I have all this training in jazz. I don't want to let go of that."

"But they said — "

"They said they want us to be great dancers," Sam says.

"Great classical dancers," I correct, wondering how anyone could have the energy to take more classes than we're already scheduled for.

Climbing the metal stairs to the third-floor studio, we can hear loud staccato drum and piano music. Sam does a little sharp-edged jazz movement on each of the last four steps before we enter the small waiting room. "Hi, Lydia," she says to the woman at the desk.

Lydia looks up at Sam with a big smile. "Hey, it's our little ballerina from Boston. How you doing, Samantha?"

"I'm good. I wondered if the fall schedule is ready."

Lydia hands Sam a yellow Xeroxed sheet and smiles around at Beth, Olga, and me. "And you girls?"

My right foot is keeping beat to the music, but I say, "No, thank you."

The door to the studio opens, and a stream of sweaty, noisy dancers come into the reception area. They're not dressed in pink tights and black leotards, but in all sorts of colorful combinations of dance and street clothes. The only thing their outfits have in common is that they cling to their bodies with sweat. Sam gets a friendly welcome from Al, and a hug from one of the older girls who remembers her from last summer.

A few minutes later we're at the ballet bookstore, pooling our money for two big posters. The first one we agree on is of Patricia Gordon as Princess Aurora in *The Sleeping Beauty*. She's all in white, on *pointe*, her arms extended to the side — strong and gracefully bowed. We decide the second poster should be a male dancer. We pick out one of Mikhail Baryshnikov — a dancer who defected from Russia. In the poster he's suspended in midair with his arms extended and his legs scissor-straight.

"We still like Baryshnikov in Russia," Olga explains, "even though he left our country to live in America."

"He does very good jazz dancing, too," Sam tells Olga. "See, a lot of classical dancers do different kinds of dancing. It keeps them —"

"— on their toes," Sam and Beth say in unison.

Olga looks confused. "Dancers in America do jazz dance in toe shoes?" she asks.

It takes all the way to the studio for me to explain to Olga that there is another meaning to "on your toes."

Three

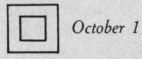 *October 1*

Dear Carole,

Hi, hi, hi. I can't believe it's only been three weeks since I left Oregon. Your letter was great. I'm sorry I haven't written before, but I've hardly had a minute to myself. Right now (as I write this) I'm sitting in my bed writing to you with a flashlight. I mean writing to you with a pen by the light of a flashlight.

There's so much I want to tell you about what it's like here. We have two schedules — the schedule of a full-time dance student with three dance classes a day, plus the schedule of a normal

23

student with eighth-grade academic classes at the Professional Children's Public School (PCPS). You were right about the kids at PCPS — lots of them are movie stars and models that we've seen on TV and in the movies.

Tammy Schneider is in my math class. She's even cuter in real life than in the TV series, and she seems like a normal kid. She's not very good in math, though, probably because she spends so much time being an actress.

The "NBS bunheads" — that's what they call us — are so busy going back and forth between the National Ballet School and PCPS, we can't really get to be friends with the other kids.

This is how it goes. From 8:30 to 10:00 we take math and English at PCPS, then rush over to the studio for dance class at 10:30. We grab a lunch on the way back to PCPS. Usually we get a sandwich and yogurt at a deli. Sometimes we stop for a slice of pizza.

After lunch we take social studies and science. By then it's 2:00 and time to rush back over to the studio for another dance class — on pointe. Then there's a study hour in the dressing room, before our final dance class of the day. Sometimes I fall asleep during study hour.

Back at the house we take showers and eat dinner together. Then we have an hour of recreation in the living room when we're allowed to watch TV. Mostly we sew ribbons on our ballet slippers and toe shoes and complain about our aches and pains. We have two more hours in our rooms to do homework before bed, but I'm usually out like a light before it's time for "lights out." It's hard to stay awake to study when you've taken so many dance classes.

My roommate, Olga, is from Russia. You'd really like her. She can speak English very well. I know about one word in Russian — nyet, which means "no." One of our teachers and Saki — the head of the whole ballet company — are Russian, too, so Olga gets to yak it up in her own language with them. She told me what it's like to live in Russia. There aren't many radios, TVs, computers, or just about anything that you plug in. And it's hard to shop for food. A lot of the time her mother has to stand in a long line just to get bread and then go to another line for meat. Oh, yeah, and there isn't much toilet paper. Isn't that disgusting? Olga's idea of a good time is to walk around a store saying, "so many things" and squeeze six-packs of soft toilet paper.

Writing to you is making me homesick for everything at home, so I'd better stop.

Your best friend,

Kate

P.S.   There's this guy who lives with us — the son of the housemother — who's sort of nice, but mostly he tries too hard to be funny. His friends are always coming around here to see the "bunheads." They're all sort of juvenile.

Four

I sit down next to Sam under the *barre* in Studio Three and tell her, "I don't think I can make it through another class." Just the thought of class with Ms. Hayden makes my muscles ache.

"I took classes all summer so this wouldn't happen, but I still ache," Sam tells us. "I hurt in muscles I never knew I had."

Beth comes into the studio and plunks down beside us. "Just one more class today," she reminds us. She points with her chin to the other side of the room. "Look at Lyrice."

We all watch silently as Lyrice and several other older girls stretch to warm up for class.

Beth stands and slides her leg along the *barre*. "Might as well get started," she says.

At four-thirty on the dot Ms. Hayden strides into the studio shouting, "Up, up, up." She glares at her students sitting under the *barre*. "This isn't a sitting room. It's a dance studio. You should warm up your bodies while you wait for the instructor."

Forty-five minutes later, halfway through jumps, Ms. Hayden asks, "Where is the *energy*? What is wrong with you girls?"

Olga answers for all of us. "The first week of classes after vacation is very hard on a dancer. This happens in Russia, too."

"Of course, it's difficult," Ms. Hayden scolds as she paces in front of us. "I know that. But you must not show the difficulty in your dancing. One lesson you must learn early in your training is how to work through the difficult days. If a dancer is tired, she doesn't let the audience see her fatigue. If she is in pain, she doesn't let the audience see that pain." She looks around at us. I wish I could sit down for this lecture. "A muscle that aches can still extend the leg. You must learn to work through the pain and fatigue. Do you know what the dancer's motto is?" she asks.

Lyrice raises her hand.

"Yes, Lyrice."

"No pain. No gain."

"That is correct," Ms. Hayden tells her. "In unison now. What is the motto of the dancer?"

We all reply, "No pain. No gain."

"Now," she nods to the pianist, "we will jump with energy."

That night my sore leg muscles have little energy left for climbing the two flights of stairs to my bedroom. As I walk across the second-floor landing, Jason whispers to me from a crack in his bedroom door, "Hey, Kate, where are you going?"

"Upstairs," I whisper back and start up the second flight of stairs, one painful step at a time.

"Come on in," he whispers after me.

I turn and whisper back, "Jason, why are we whispering?"

"Come on in," he repeats.

I've never been in Jason's room because he keeps the door shut all the time and there's a handpainted orange-and-black sign that says "Private Property — Beware of Guard Dog." Who would want to go in his room, anyway?

"I've got homework," I tell him. "Besides" — I point to his ugly sign — "I can read."

Sam appears behind Jason and signals me to come in. She has a mischievous grin spread across her face that I can't resist. I go into Jason's room. It's so tiny that Sam and I have to sit on his unmade bed before he can close the door. I look around. The only other furniture is a small desk and straight-back chair. There's no room for a bureau, so he must have to keep all his clothes in the closet or under the bed.

He sits on the edge of his desk.

"What's going on?" I ask Sam.

"We're going out. To meet Jason's friends — Charlie and Ira — at Mario's Pizza."

"Did your mother say we could go?" I ask Jason.

"She won't know," Jason answers. Then he does this amazing imitation of his mother: "Do not bring that Charles and Ira around here to socialize with my dancers, young man. It will interrupt their discipline and concentration." Jason drops back to his own voice. "So I'm not bringing them here. I'm bringing you to them. Besides, Mom's not here for us to ask."

"Or to see us go out," Sam puts in.

"If she's not here," I wonder out loud, "why are we whispering?"

"Because Ginny and Lyrice might tell," Jason explains.

Sam says, "Beth knows, but she's going to stay here and rest her knee."

"What about Olga?" I ask.

"She's invited, too," Jason says. "She'll love it."

Jason's right about Olga. "It's fun to be out at night," she tells me as we walk behind Sam and Jason toward Mario's. "All the lights and people. I want to be with normal American teenagers, not just dancers."

"I don't know how normal Jason's friends are," I tell her. "And what if Ruth gets home before we do? How are we going to sneak back in without getting caught? She'll be furious. She might even send us home."

"Don't worry," Olga says. "We'll be in bed like sleeping dolls when she comes home."

"Regular sleeping beauties," Sam says over her shoulder.

"That's my favorite ballet," I tell them.

Jason and Sam wait to walk on either side of Olga and me. Jason says, "You guys are going to see *The Sleeping Beauty* tomorrow night. I heard my mother talking on the phone with the box office after dinner. She probably wants to surprise you."

Olga and Sam and I are so excited about going to see the ballet that we jump up and down and do leaps over the Broadway sidewalk between 70th and 69th Streets. "We'll see Patricia Gordon dance," I shout at the height of a leap.

In a flash we're at Mario's, sitting in a booth with Jason, Ira, and Charlie. They can't get over how excited we are about going to a ballet.

"I can tell a ballet dancer from a block away," Charlie says. He puts two pieces of pizza on the bare table and, pretending they're feet, he "walks them" the length of the table in turn-out.

Four girls in the booth next to ours start giggling like crazy. So do Jason and Ira.

"Nice friends, Jason," Sam says. She takes one of the slices from Charlie and starts to eat it. "Did you ask us here to make fun of us?"

"They're just teasing," Jason says.

So then we tease them about their crazy haircuts. Charlie's black hair has a streak of blond in the front. Ira's light brown hair has gooky stuff in it to make it stand on end. And I accuse Jason of getting his curls from a permanent, which he denies like crazy.

Even though he knows the answer, Charlie asks Olga, "What do you call that thing you do with your hair, all bunched up in the back like that?"

"In English, 'bun,' " says Olga, proudly turning her head to show them her bun.

"Bun?" Charlie says. "Bun. Bun. Bunheads who live in a BUNstone. Get it. Brownstone, bunstone." Sam and Olga think it's funny. They're all having a good time. But I'm not having much fun. I'm too worried that if Ruth discovers we snuck out she won't let us go to *The Sleeping Beauty.*

When we're walking across the green-and-white tile floor at Mario's, I force my feet into parallel but it feels awkward. Once we're on the sidewalk, we run all the way back to the "bunstone," feet pointing whichever way they move fastest.

We're home before Ruth! Olga and I are running up the stairs to our bedroom when I see Lyrice coming out of our bathroom. She's wiping her mouth with a tissue. Was she throwing up again?

I'm trying to decide which question to ask her — "Are you sick?" or "Why don't you use your own bathroom?" — when she asks us, "Where *were* you two? I thought you were both in bed."

"We were — ah — in the kitchen," I say.

"Ugh," she says as she passes us. "You smell like a pizza parlor." She smells like throwup, but I don't say it. She says, "You were in Mario's kitchen, not Ruth's kitchen. You'll pay for it tomorrow."

"Don't tell Ruth," Olga says.

"I'd never do that," Lyrice tells her. "I'm just saying that you'll be bushed for ten o'clock class. Saki's our teacher tomorrow, you know." She stares right at me when she adds, "I am not a tattletale."

When we're in our room Olga asks me, "What kind of animal is a tattle? What kind of a tail does a tattle have?"

I tell her that "tattle" isn't an animal and explain what tattletale means. Then she wants to go over the different spellings and meanings of "tail" and "tale." Next she wants to review other English synonyms. I remember "pale" and "pail." She thinks of "sale" and "sail." Then it's "male" and "mail." I think of "vale" and "veil," but have to explain the difference in spelling from the other pairs (pears) of words we've done. Finally she stops asking me questions about words that sound alike but have different meanings and falls asleep. But I don't. The pizza slices have become a heavy glob in my stomach. I lie awake looking around the dark room.

How can I sleep when I'm so worried that I'll be too tired to be good for Saki's class?

"At the *barre*, my little beauties," Saki tells us when we come into the studio the next morning. It's Saturday, so the whole day will be devoted to three dance classes without the interruption of going over to PCPS. In the evening we'll attend *The Sleeping Beauty*.

As I position myself for first position *pliés*,

instead of a clump of pizza rolling around in my stomach there are butterflies of nervousness flitting around.

"Tuck, tuck, Miss Oregon. Please — the posture, the stomach."

The pianist — Mr. Berkow — plays the opening bars of music. I pull myself up straighter and tuck in my bottom so my stomach will fit into the right place. We begin.

"Miss California. Deeper. Deeper on the *pliés*," Saki commands Beth.

When he corrects Olga, he speaks in Russian. The third time he does this she speaks back to him — in English. "I understand class in English very well," she tells him. "The other teachers speak to me in English."

He answers her again in Russian. This time sternly.

For floor work Mr. Berkow plays Tchaikovsky's score from *The Sleeping Beauty*. Combinations, turns, and leaps are all done to the same music that the company will dance to when we see them perform on stage in just a few hours.

When we're back in the dressing room I ask Beth, "How's your knee?" I can barely see her from the sweat seeping into my eyes. "Maybe you shouldn't have taken class."

She's wiping the sweat from her own brow. "I'm working it out," she tells me as she sits down on the bench between the rows of lockers. "I've got to keep dancing." She rubs her knee and then stretches it out. She tries to cover up a wince of pain with a smile and says, "You know what Ms. Hayden says: 'No pain. No gain.'"

Five

At seven that evening I'm zipping up the back of Olga's best dress. "Your dress is beautiful," I tell her. "And your hair is so blonde and wavy. You look gorgeous."

"You, too," Olga tells me. Olga's silky dress is the same light blue color as her eyes. My dress is cream-colored satin with a big, white lace collar. Both have full skirts.

"We could be onstage for the Christmas party in *The Nutcracker* ballet dressed just like this," I tell her as I connect the hook and eye on her collar.

"Last year," she tells me, "I was Marie in *The*

Nutcracker with the Kirov Ballet. We performed it with Saki's choreography."

"What did he say to you in class today when you told him to correct you in English?"

"That he will speak to me in whatever language he wants to. That my job is to understand and to dance as he tells me, not to tell him how to speak." She sighs. "Dance teachers at the Bolshoi Ballet school act like big bosses, too."

Sam pops into our room to see if we're ready. "Ohhh," she says. "You two look so pretty."

"Wow!" I tell her. "You look so — so — amazing."

"Like a rock-and-roll star in Russia," Olga comments.

Instead of a girlie party dress, Sam's wearing a black-and-gold-toned, striped Lycra miniskirt over a black unitard. At least two dozen black and gold bracelets hang around her wrists. Her hair's loose, wild, and kinky instead of in the neat little braids she usually wraps around her head into a barrette.

"Is Beth ready?" I ask.

"I'm ready," Beth says. She's come in behind Sam, dressed like Olga and me — proper girls on their way to a special party. We meet Lyrice and Ginny in the living room. They look pretty grown up in their best outfits, but not wild looking like Sam. They *ooh* and *ahh* about how great Sam looks.

Ruth comes in and looks us over. Her gaze stops for a shocked second on Sam, but she calmly tells us, "Lovely, lovely. Now stand like dancers."

Ruth walks down the front steps between Sam and me. "Perhaps, Samantha," she says, "the next time we go to the ballet, you might like to borrow a party dress from one of the others. I'm sure Kate has an extra little something she'd lend you."

"I have a party dress like that," Sam says. "My mother likes it better than this outfit, too. I'll wear it another time, okay?"

"Yes, of course," Ruth answers. When Ruth's moved on ahead of us, Sam raises her eyebrows and smiles at me.

"I'd much rather be wearing what you have on than what I have on," I tell her. "If I dared."

"Don't worry, Kate," she says. "Ruth didn't hurt my feelings. That's just the way she is." She jumps over the last step. "And this is the way I am."

Ruth ignores Charlie, Ira, and Jason, who are skateboarding behind us the half block up to Broadway, but Sam and I hang back at the end of our group to talk to them. When we say good-bye at the corner, Charlie comments on our loose hairstyles. "I guess you left all your buns in the bunstone," he says with a laugh.

"Enough with the buns," Sam says. "It's getting boring."

Ira's laughing so hard at Charlie's corny comment that he falls off his skateboard and lands flat on the sidewalk, right on his bottom.

"Maybe you guys should worry about your own buns," I call over my shoulder as we cross the street to catch up with the others.

When the curtain goes up on the set of *The Sleeping Beauty,* I go into a trance. I've never seen anything so beautiful in my entire life. Everything about it is perfect — the music, the set, the costumes, the dancers. But the most perfect thing about it is Patricia Gordon as Princess Aurora. I try to imagine what it would feel like to be onstage — turning, leaping, dancing. Part of me knows what hard work it is, how I'd sweat and ache and be nervous about making a mistake or falling and injuring myself. But when it's my turn to use the binoculars and I study Patricia Gordon's face, I think, she's not Patricia Gordon, she's Princess Aurora awakening from a hundred-year sleep to see her Prince.

"Come on," Ruth says to us above the applause

and cheers of the last curtain call. "We're going backstage."

"This is your chance to get an autograph," Sam whispers as we weave through the crowds leaving the theater.

We reach the door that leads backstage and go down the stairs to the big dressing room for the *corps de ballet* dancers. The dancers don't pay any attention to us, but some of them know Ruth and chat with her. We stand near the door watching them getting out of costumes, removing makeup, using the phones, and drinking sodas. There's a big portable radio on a stool in the middle of the room tuned to a hot rock-and-roll station.

I step back into the hall and immediately see who I'm looking for — Patricia Gordon. She's holding the flowers that were presented to her during her curtain call and is walking toward her own dressing room at the end of the corridor.

I run after her, calling, "Could I have your autograph?"

She turns and sees me. I can't believe I yelled like that. But she smiles — just at me. "Sure," she says. "Here, hold these." She hands me her bouquet of roses and baby's breath. I take the flowers and hand her my program to autograph.

That's when I realize that I don't have anything for her to write with. "I don't have a pen," I explain.

I'm surprised at how thick and phony her stage makeup looks close up. Streaks of sweat glisten around her eyes and down her neck. I wonder what it feels like to wear false eyelashes.

"I must have a pen in my dressing room," she tells me.

"You were wonderful," I blurt out as I follow her into the little room. "You're my favorite dancer, but I never saw you dance before tonight. Except on television once, and in *Dance Magazine*."

She laughs at my stupid comment, then rummages through the makeup stuff on her dressing table, looking for a pen. I look around the room — there are bouquets of flowers everywhere. Roses. Lilacs. Lilies. The sweet smells remind me of my grandmother's funeral.

Patricia holds up an eyebrow pencil. "I'll use this," she says. "What's your name?"

"Kate Conway. I'm a dancer, too. A student, really, with the National Ballet School."

"I know," she says.

"You do?"

"Sure. You look like an NBS student. All intense and wiry and serious."

"Most people say they can tell because of the way I walk."

"Have they chosen the children's parts for *The Nutcracker* yet?" she asks.

"We try out on Monday," I answer.

"I'm dancing The Sugar Plum Fairy. Maybe we'll be dancing together."

Oh, boy, I think, if I'm a Candy Cane or a Marzipan Candy, I'll be dancing with The Sugar Plum Fairy. "I hope so," I tell her.

She finishes writing and hands me back my program.

I thank her, say good-bye, and take in the details of her dressing room as I leave. A pair of dungarees and a turtleneck sweater are hanging on a hook. I wish I could see her when all the makeup is off and she's in her street clothes. What will she do now? I wonder. Does she have a date with an exciting man — like Prince Charming? Or dinner with some other famous dancers? I don't think she'd do either of those things in jeans. Maybe she's married. I realize I don't know anything about Patricia Gordon but her wonderful dancing.

In the hall I look down to see that I'm still holding her flowers. I go back into the dressing room. Before she sees me, I see her reflection in the mirror. She's already smeared makeup-remover cream all over her face. In all that white, her darkly made-up eyes look sad, like a clown's.

I extend the bouquet. "I forgot to give you back your flowers."

She smiles a white smile. "You keep them. For good luck in *The Nutcracker* tryouts."

When we get back home, I put the bouquet of flowers in a vase and place it in the middle of the dining room table. We're having a post-ballet "tea party," but Ruth is the only one drinking tea. The rest of us are having milk and apple juice with the éclairs and brownies that Alice made for us. Ginny puts the score of *The Sleeping Beauty* on the CD player, and we're all talking at once about how much we loved the ballet.

"Patricia Gordon is such a magnificent dancer," Ruth comments.

"I would do anything to be able to dance like that," Lyrice says.

"Anything?" Sam asks.

"Yes," Lyrice says. "Anything. That's what it takes. Total dedication."

"She's right, Samantha," Ruth says. "If you don't give it everything you've got, you can't achieve it. There wasn't one dancer on that stage tonight who doesn't put dance first, above all else. But everything they endure makes it worth it. I hope everyone here is doing that. Putting

44

dance first. Ginny Lee, are you?"

"Oh, yes. My mother says I was born dancing. I love it, everything about it. I can't imagine doing anything else with my life."

"Dance is always important to me," Olga says. "I've worked for many years to be a good dancer. You have to love it or you couldn't do it."

"I love to dance," Sam says. "I think about it all the time. And even though I like to do lots of kinds of dance, ballet is my first love."

Before Beth and I have a chance to say how we feel, the front door opens and closes. It's Jason, back from the movies. "Hey," he yells from the hallway, "are we having a party?" When he sees the pile of éclairs and brownies on the table, he says, "Yes, we are having a party. A very good party." He pulls up a chair and smiles around at us. "How's it going? What are you all so serious about?"

"Your mother was just saying that you can't be a dancer without it being the most important thing in your life," Ginny tells him.

Jason swallows a big bite of chocolate éclair before saying, "Mom could have been a great dancer. She *was* a great dancer until I came along and spoiled it."

"I made a choice," Ruth says. "If I had it to do over again, I might do something different."

We all stop eating and become totally silent.

I can't believe Ruth said that if she had to do it over again she might not have Jason. Mostly I can't believe she said it right in front of Jason.

"Oh, I don't mean that I'm not happy I had a child," Ruth continues, breaking the silence. "I mean I shouldn't have given up dance so quickly. I should have had Jason later when I finished my performance career."

"But he'd have been a different kid if you'd had him later — especially if he'd had a different father," Sam says.

"And, now, Jason — or whoever he turned out to be — would only be like two years old or something," Lyrice says as she reaches for a second éclair.

"*Goo-goo, ga-ga,*" Jason gurgles and we all laugh.

"My goodness, Lyrice," Ruth says, changing the subject, "I don't know how you can eat so much and stay so wonderfully slender. Every cookie I ate when I was a dancer went right to my waistline. It still does."

I watch Lyrice gobble down the éclair, already eyeing the pile of brownies.

Ruth smiles at her. "You're a lucky girl," she says.

I put down my éclair. My stomach goes queasy. I think I know why Lyrice can eat so much and not gain weight.

That night I stay awake on purpose. When I hear a creak from the staircase, I get out of bed and go stand close to the bathroom door where I listen to the gagging coughs of throwing up followed by the flush of the toilet.

Sam's voice wakes me up the next morning. "Hey, you guys, you ever getting up?"

I pretend I'm still asleep.

She bounces on my bed. "Come on, lazybones. Don't waste the day. It's already ten o'clock. Let's go to the park or something."

"Ruth said we can sleep in on Sundays. So I'm staying in bed until Monday," I tell her.

Beth comes into our room. "Let's help Kate get up," she tells Sam. The two of them are on my bed, tickling and pulling to get me up.

"No. I won't get up," I shout. "You can't make me." Out of the corner of my eye I can see Olga trying to decide whether to stay comfy under her covers or get up and join in my persecution.

Beth starts dancing and gesturing like the prince in *The Sleeping Beauty* as she chants, "I am Prince Charming. You must wake up from your hundred-year sleep, princess. I will marry you, and we will live happily ever after." She ends with three jumps and swoops down on one knee in a bow before me. We're still applauding when she suddenly rolls on the floor, wincing in pain and grabbing her bent knee. "Oh, no," she cries.

"Is it your bad knee?" I ask Beth.

She nods.

"I'll get Ruth," Sam tells us.

"It'll be okay," I tell Beth. "Just stay there, don't move." I pull the blanket from my bed and put it over her. Olga is patting the tears off Beth's cheeks and trying to soothe her. But the tears keep coming. Her face is white and pinched with pain.

"It hurts so much," she whispers to me. "How will I dance? Please, don't let them send me home."

That's what we're all afraid of, that they'll send Beth home. But a few hours later, when she's come back from getting X rays and seeing the doctor, no one says anything about going home.

"She has to stay off her knee for a week, and then we'll see how it is," Ruth tells us at lunch. We all know that means Beth won't be dancing in *The Nutcracker* ballet.

This is the first day I'm seriously homesick. It gets really bad when my parents make their weekly phone call to me at seven o'clock. We have four phones in my house in Oregon, so everyone is on a phone, talking at once.

"I miss you sweetie. How are you feeling?" That's my mother.

"Your mother's holding up. Don't you worry about her." That's my father.

"When you coming home? I miss you, too." That's Judy.

"You said you were glad Kate was gone because you get to play in her room." That's Tommy, talking to Judy.

"Shut up, dummy," Judy yells at Tommy.

"We're all very proud of you, Kate," my mom says. "Everyone asks about you, like you're a celebrity."

"Are you coming home for Christmas?" Tommy asks.

"Not if I get a part in *The Nutcracker*," I tell him.

"Oh," Judy says sadly. "I hope you don't get a part, then."

"Will you be Marie and wear a stupid nightgown onstage?" Tommy asks.

"She's too old to play Marie," my mother explains.

"Don't you worry, Judy, your Katie will be home for a nice long visit starting New Year's Eve," my father says.

After I hang up, I stare at the phone and

think, it's a long time until December thirty-first.

When we go to bed that night, I ask Olga, "Are you homesick?"

"My home is healthy," she tells me. "No one sick."

Because homesick tears are beginning to slide down my cheeks, and my throat is tight with homesickness, I don't even try to explain to Olga what homesick really means in English. I fall asleep crying.

Six

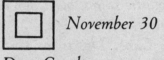 *November 30*

Dear Carole,

Something sad has happened in our house. Beth has a knee injury that isn't getting better, so they're sending her home for an operation. We all feel awful for her.

The other news is that everyone else in my house got good parts in The Nutcracker *ballet. In Act One, I'm a mouse. You wouldn't believe how fabulous my costume is. I have this big round body made of gray fake fur, and a mouse-head that I put on separately. The head is so big that I look out of the mouth. It took awhile to get used to dancing with all* of that on my body. When the Nutcracker kills the Mouse King, and the mice carry him off stage, I walk behind the body, crying and rubbing my eyes. But really I'm rubbing where my own forehead is, since that's where the mouse costume eyes are. I understand how the sad little mouse feels. Even though the Mouse King was evil, she believed in him and loved him. I figure, as the mouse, that I don't know any other way but the ways of the Mouse King. If I had been born a toy soldier, I would be on the side of good. But because I was born a mouse, all I've known is the ways of the mice, which in this story are evil ways. I really don't know about anything else but to follow the Mouse King. Sam is a toy soldier in that scene. She pokes at me with a hard plastic sword, but I don't feel it because of my fat costume.

In Act Two, I'm a Candy Cane. This is the part of the story when Marie, as the Little Princess, and Herr Drosselmeier's nephew, as the Little Prince, go to The Land of Sweets. I know it sounds silly to be a Candy Cane, but it isn't really. We wear white satin pants and tops decorated with pink and green ribbons sewn round and round the costume. Hundreds of little bells are sewn on the ribbons so we jingle when we dance. We carry big striped hoops that match our costumes. The dance was hard to learn and is strenuous to do because it has lots of jumps and leaps — some of them through the hoops.

I don't know if I'll have time to write during this

next month because of all the dancing in The Nutcracker.

Olga's a Candy Cane, too. Sam is a Marzipan. She's the youngest one to get that part. That's what a great dancer she is. Hardly any of us knew what marzipan candy was, so our housemother gave us all a piece of marzipan to eat so we'd know what it tasted like. It's okay, but not great. You can do neat things with marzipan because it has the consistency of Play-Doh, so people put food coloring in it and mold it into different shapes. The ones we ate were little candy canes, which was a funny coincidence for those of us who are Candy Canes in the ballet. I think marzipan looks prettier than it tastes.

Thank you for the great, long letter. I wish I'd been with you for the eighth-grade camping trip into the mountains. It sounds like a great adventure with the surprise snowstorm and everything. Remember how we always said we wanted to go camping in the snow? Now you've done it.

Boy, do I ever miss Oregon. There are trees in New York, but they're mostly in Central Park and I hardly ever have time to go there. Maybe my mother will take us for a ride into the mountains when I come home for vacation. I'll be there on New Year's Eve. I can't wait to see you.

Gotta go. Tell all the kids that I like in our class hello for me and that I miss them. Actually, I'm getting so homesick that I'm beginning to miss people

I don't even like, so you might as well say hello to everyone for me.

Your best friend,

Kate the Mouse

P.S.   I'm going to wear false eyelashes when I dance as the Candy Cane. So is Olga. We're not going to tell anyone, we're just going to do it.

P.P.S.   I saw the Macy's Thanksgiving Day parade in real life. It was cold. The balloons are really big. I think they should have a Nutcracker balloon and maybe one of the mice.

Seven

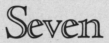 The first thing I think when I wake up is, today I dance in *The Nutcracker*. At the breakfast table we're all talking about it. "Three thousand people!" Sam exclaims.

"That's six thousand eyes watching us dance tonight," Olga says. We stop talking when we hear Beth coming. Today is also the day that Beth is going home. From where I sit, I can see her coming down the stairs. First she puts her cane on the step below her. Then one foot goes down. Then, very carefully, the second foot follows. One, two, three — for each painfully taken stair. I remember how she used to dash down those stairs two at a time.

Sam leans over and whispers to me, "She cried all night."

Beth limps into the room on her cane. She looks pale and sad.

Olga gets up and goes over to her. "Oh, Beth," she says. "Please stay friends and write me many letters."

Jason says, "Hey, Beth, real life isn't so bad. Just think of all the time you'll have to do normal things, like hang out with great kids like me. And, man, living in California in the winter. That must be the greatest. Maybe you'll become an actor."

Ruth gives Jason a quick glance that means shut up, and says to Beth, "Dear, sit next to me." Beth does it. Ruth puts an arm around her and squeezes her close. "You're still young. You have the desire to dance and a great talent for it. After the operation you will build up your strength again. You have time, my dear."

I know that what Ruth is saying isn't true because I heard her and Saki talking in the hall outside my bedroom. Saki told Ruth, "She'll always have trouble with that knee, even after surgery."

Soon we're all crying and saying good-bye to Beth. She forces a smile and thanks us all for being so good to her. "Have a wonderful time onstage tonight," she says. "You'll all be great dancers." As Ruth is getting in the cab to take Beth to the airport, I hear her tell Beth again that she can still become a ballerina.

Later, when Sam and I are walking over to the theater for our first performance of *The Nutcracker,* I ask her, "Why did Ruth lie to Beth like that?"

"To give her some hope, I suppose."

"I think it's better to be honest."

"Beth is pretty upset," Sam says.

"She loves dancing even more than I do," I tell Sam as we cross the wide slushy street of honking cars and bustling pedestrians to get to the theater.

No Christmas tree is as wonderful as the Christmas tree on the stage for the first act of *The Nutcracker.* The ballet opens with a family party in an old-fashioned house with high ceilings, so the tree is already bigger than any tree I've ever seen in a house.

When Marie falls asleep on the couch, Herr Drosselmeier comes in and performs some magic and everything in the room starts to "grow." I watch from the wings with the other mice when, in a flash of light, the window goes from being normal-sized to being as big as a house. I see the tree grow by rising up out of the stage floor, and what was the whole tree just a minute before ends up being only the very top part of it. The audience goes *"ooh"* and *"ahh"* while the tree is growing, and applauds like crazy when it's finished. By the time I'm onstage as a mouse, the tree is mighty big. It's a brightly lit tree loaded down with decorations and toys that are as big as me.

In the wings, before I go onstage, I feel big and awkward in my mouse costume. But once I'm onstage near the tree, I feel like I *am* a tiny mouse. And by the time we're in battle with the Nutcracker and the toy soldiers, it's as if Marie shrunk to the size of her toys, and we are really mice having a battle with toys that have come to life.

When I come offstage, I stop in the wings to watch the tree ascend into the ceiling and disappear while the staging for the snow scene descends behind it. Then the snow starts to fall. It looks just like real snow. The *corps de ballet,* in white "snowflake" costumes, dance out of the wings onto the snowy stage. Their dance is beautiful and exciting. Soon a chorus of voices join the musicians to make the sounds of swirling snow as more and more of it falls on the dancers and on the stage floor.

I'm thinking of what Beth is missing and how she might never dance again, when someone pulls on my tail. I turn around. It's Sam in her toy soldier costume.

"Take off your mouse-head," she says. I look around. The other mice have taken off their heads and put them on the special mouse costume rack and have already gone down to the dressing rooms to get ready for the second act. I take my head off and place it next to the other mouse-heads on the rack while Sam watches the "Dance of the Snowflakes." "Hurry," she whispers over her shoulder.

I envy the stagehand who cues the tree and snow. He gets to watch this wonderful dance over and over, while I have to leave it.

On the elevator going down I tell Sam, "You were great. I was really afraid of you."

"I was afraid of you, too," she says.

"But you knew you were going to win," I tell her.

"I don't think of that when I'm dancing the part," she tells me. "I pretend it's happening for the first time. I really was afraid."

The elevator doors open. One of the dressing room helpers meets us. "Let's go, girls," she says. "It was a great first act. Now let's move it."

Lyrice is already at our end of the dressing table applying her makeup. She was a mouse, too. And, like Sam, she'll be a Marzipan in the second act.

The dressing room is just like the one that the *corps de ballet* uses. Only we have a lot of volunteer helpers, like some of the mothers of NBS students who live in New York City.

The dressing room tables are chock full of boxes of candies and cookies. Bunches of balloons are tied to the corners of mirrors, and there are bouquets of flowers everywhere. All gifts for us — the young dancers in *The Nutcracker*.

"Here," Lyrice says, handing me a long white box tied with a big red bow. "These came for you." I pull a small pink card out of its envelope and read, " 'To our star ballerina. Love, Mr. Randolph and the students of the Portland Ballet Institute.' " I open the box to see a dozen long-stemmed red roses. "They're from my ballet teacher," I tell Lyrice and Sam. "He used to dance with this company." I feel like a real star as I take a deep breath of the sweet rose scent.

I put the flower box next to my dance bag and reach for a piece of chocolate-covered caramel. The costume mistress, Madame Minoff, shakes her index finger at me. "No, no," she scolds. "No candy. And only a little after the performance. I'm not altering costumes." She claps her hands. The excited chatter of dancers and helpers stops. Madame Minoff is very strict, and we are afraid of her. She's made and cared for the costumes for *The Nutcracker* for thirty years, so she knows everything about the ballet and is very particular about how everything should be done. "I do not make costumes bigger during *The Nutcracker.* No. No. The day I let out a costume — even one-half inch — is the day I put red-hot pepper sauce on every sweet that enters this dressing room. Understood?"

"Yes, Madame Minoff," we answer in unison. Even the mothers say it. I pat my belly. Still hard and flat. I look down at my chest. Still pretty flat, too. I'm safe.

Ginny stuffs a chocolate in her mouth. "For energy," she tells me.

Madame Minoff gives her a quick glare as she passes behind us, but it's to Lyrice that she says, "Stand up. Let me see."

Lyrice obeys. Madame Minoff's old crooked fingers poke and pull at Lyrice's costume, especially around her waist. "You," she says, "*should* eat chocolates. I'm going to have to pull this one in. Come to me after the performance."

"You're so lucky," Sam tells Lyrice when Madame Minoff has moved on to persecute someone else. "No one ever tells me to eat." Sam hands her the box of chocolates.

"No, thanks," Lyrice says. "Not before I dance."

"You hardly ate any dinner," Sam says. "I always think you eat more than any of us — especially sweets. Then sometimes you don't eat anything at all."

"I wasn't hungry," Lyrice says. "I'll make up for it later."

"Ten minutes to curtain," a voice booms from the loudspeaker. No more talking and eating. It's time to hurry.

Two weeks later, I'm onstage for my fifteenth performance as a Candy Cane. My face hurts from smiling while the other candies and the Teas dance. And my body aches from staying in one position for so long. I daydream about what I'll eat after the performance, and I count up the money I've made so far for dancing in *The Nutcracker*. I count fifteen performances, which adds up to $150. The musical introduction for the Candy Canes begins. We're dancing, but my mind still wanders. I remember that last December my mother brought home two big boxes of candy canes for our Christmas tree. I wonder what the tree looks like this year and what it will be like to be in New York City for Christmas instead of in Eugene, Oregon, with my family.

When we've finished the routine and I'm again frozen in position watching the other dancers, I study Patricia Gordon — The Sugar Plum

Fairy — who also stands to watch the other dancers. I wonder what she's thinking about.

After the last curtain call we all head for the elevators. For the first time since we started in *The Nutcracker,* I'm on the same elevator as Patricia Gordon. She doesn't notice me because she's already untying her pink satin toe shoes. By the time the elevator doors open at the third floor, she's taken them off. As she walks down the hall in her stocking feet, she slaps the toe shoes against one another and I hear her scolding them angrily, "Bad, bad shoes." She throws them in the trash can and limps off. I see a bright red spot of blood leaking through the toe of her tights.

Later, on the way out of the theater, I lag behind my friends so I can grab that pair of toe shoes from the trash can. I slip them into my opened dance bag, zip it closed, and rush to catch up with the others.

Even though we're dead tired when we get home, Ginny, Sam, Olga, and I sit on Beth's empty bed and talk. We stretch our legs out in V shapes around a box of cookies that we're devouring. Dancing makes you hungry.

I'm showing them Patricia's toe shoes. "Look inside the right one," I tell Sam.

"That's wild," she says as she peers into the

63

shoe. "I can see the bloodstain." She hands it to Ginny. "Look."

When I have the toe shoes back, I look again at the dark spot of blood. It tells me that Patricia Gordon was feeling pain while The Sugar Plum Fairy was smiling so sweetly at her audience onstage and in the theater.

"It's funny that I love having her shoes so much and she hated them," I say.

"They didn't fit right," Ginny says.

Olga says, "I hate my shoes sometimes, too. Sometimes I even hate my body when it won't do what I want."

"Me, too," Sam admits. "Especially when it gets too fat." She puts back the cookie that she'd just taken.

"Is that what Lyrice is afraid of?" I ask them. "Getting fat?" No one answers. I wonder, do they know that Lyrice makes herself throw up? Should I tell them?

Ginny finally says, "We're all afraid of getting fat. Everyone knows that Saki wouldn't renew our scholarships if we gained too much weight. But don't you think Lyrice is weirder than the rest of us, the way she doesn't eat and then stuffs herself?"

"How come she's losing weight if she stuffs herself?" I ask quietly.

No one says anything for a few seconds. Then

Sam answers in a whisper, "Because she makes herself throw up. I've heard her."

"Me, too," I say. I'm glad that I'm not the only one who knows.

I wonder if Ginny knew before we told her. She pulls her legs into herself and hugs them. She looks up at us sadly. "I thought maybe she was doing that, but I tried not to think about it. It's so awful. Does she do it a lot?"

"She does it in our bathroom," Sam tells her.

"A lot," I add. Then I ask the question we're all thinking: "Should we tell?"

Ginny shakes her head. "I think we should talk to Lyrice and try to get her to tell for herself." Ginny looks from Sam to me. She's only a year older than we are, but I think she's much more grown up than that.

"Let's all of us talk to her tomorrow," Olga suggests.

We agree that's what we should do.

Ginny says, "Lyrice worries about her body all the time. She's afraid that her breasts will grow big. She says she never wants to get her period."

Sam says, "Sometimes I feel that way, too. I'm afraid I'll have big breasts like my mother and then I won't look like a ballerina. I try not to feel that way, but sometimes I can't help it."

"There was a girl in the house last year,"

Ginny tells us. "Sandy. She went through puberty, and her whole body changed in one year. She looked really neat — a beautiful woman at sixteen."

"What happened to her?" I ask.

"I bet Saki kicked her out," Olga says. "Mr. Big Boss who thinks that dancers are his instruments, like the musician's violin."

Ginny says, "Maybe he would have if she hadn't left on her own. But it was her decision. She said she was sick of people telling her she should lose weight. She said she wasn't a little girl anymore, and she didn't want to look like one — or be treated like one." I think of all the ballerinas I see in the theater and at the studios, with their tight, muscular bodies and flat chests.

We hear quick steps on the stairs. "Maybe it's Lyrice," Sam says.

"Let's talk to her now and get it over with," I whisper, "before she does it again."

But it's not Lyrice. It's Ruth. She strides into the room and looks around at us sternly. "It's twenty minutes past bedtime, girls." She claps her hands. "Let's go. Off to your rooms." She looks at the box of cookies in the middle of Beth's bed and shakes her head. "Little piggies," she scolds. "I'm warning you. Be careful when you go home for vacation. Don't come back here all flabby. Your bodies are your instruments, and they must be kept in top-notch shape. I won't have any chubbettes in my house."

I want to talk back to Ruth. I want to tell her that we're growing girls. That when I'm hungry, I want to eat. That I don't want to be a little girl forever, but want to grow up and be a woman.

A leg cramp wakes me in the middle of the night. I knead it and wait for the pain to pass. When it does, I lay back listening to my stomach growling with hunger and feeling my heart aching with loneliness for my family. I think how if I were home and feeling this way, my mother would make me a cup of hot chocolate. Well, I remind myself, I'm a professional dancer now. I get paid for entertaining people at the ballet. I can get up and go downstairs and make myself a cup of hot chocolate. I put on my robe and tiptoe down the stairs because I know that if Ruth hears me, she'll send me back to my room with a scolding.

I can't find the hot chocolate mix, but there's a bar of dark chocolate in the freezer. I break half of it into little pieces and drop them into the warming milk. I watch the melting chocolate swirling through the white milk. It reminds me of the first "Snowflake" from the *corps de ballet* to come onstage for "The Dance of the Snowflakes." She's a dark-skinned African-American. During a brief solo, her ebony-colored

67

body swirls through the falling snow, like the chocolate in the white milk. Then I remember the dance of the Hot Chocolate in the ballet. Everything I do, I think, every thought I have, is connected to ballet. Will that be the way it is for the rest of my life? Won't I ever think of anything else?

When I turn away from the stove with my cup of hot chocolate, I nearly drop it from fright. I squelch a scream. It's Jason.

"Can I have some?" he asks.

"If you don't tell your mother," I tell him.

" 'Course not," he says. "What were you thinking about that I scared you so much?"

"The Hot Chocolate dance in *The Nutcracker*."

"Figures," he says.

"What would you be thinking about if you were making hot chocolate?" I ask him.

"How good it tastes. Maybe I'd wonder about the heating point chocolate reaches before it melts. I might think of the Hot Chocolate dance, too. I've seen that ballet about three thousand times."

When we're sitting at the table sipping our hot chocolates and eating peanut butter on crackers, Jason says, "How come you're up? Are you sick or something?"

"I'm homesick," I tell him. "And I don't know

if I'll make it here. Maybe I'm not a good enough dancer."

"Maybe," Jason says matter-of-factly. "Most dancers aren't. If you think about it, there are thousands of dancers who would love to be with a ballet company and can't make it. Or don't want it bad enough."

"Like your mother?" I ask.

"Oh, she wanted it bad enough," Jason says. "And she was good enough. Her mistake was falling in love with my dad and having me." Jason looks sad, too. "When I was about three years old, he left us, so I guess she feels she wasted her life."

"But she has you. Your mother loves you, Jason. She must like kids, to have us all living here like this."

"She doesn't love kids as much as she loves dancing," he tells me.

I take another sip of hot chocolate. "She does seem awfully dedicated to the ballet," I agree. "Didn't she want you to be a ballet dancer?"

"Sure. I took for a year. But I didn't like it."

"How come?"

"Every *plié* and leap I did, I knew she was watching and wondering if I had 'the gift.' "

" 'The gift?' "

"You know, all the stuff it takes to make

someone special, not just good."

"Did you have it?" I ask.

"I didn't take lessons long enough to find out. I guess I wanted to be more normal. I like to play basketball and do outdoors things like skateboard."

"Basketball's like dancing," I say.

"But, to me, basketball is a lot more fun," Jason says. Then he laughs. "See. We're talking about ballet again. Can't get away from it if you live here."

"It's like your mom's the old woman who lived in the shoe, and we're all her children and she doesn't know what to do."

"Only it's a toe shoe," he says.

Jason and I start laughing. I'm not sure what at. We try to keep from laughing out loud so his mother won't catch us up in the middle of the night, which makes us laugh even harder.

Eight

 The next day, while we're lining up at the *barre* for class, Ginny tells us, "I think Saki's coming to our class today."

Sam passes the word to the girl next to her, and it gets whispered down the line. Even though class won't start for another few minutes, twenty-four dancers start doing warmup exercises.

I'm not feeling very well and I dread the idea of Saki's critical eye going all over my body. Olga, who is two girls in front of me, is the only one of us not warming up. "Hey, Olga," I call up to her, "Saki's coming to our class."

She turns to me, her arms crossed and her

feet set firmly on the floor. "I'll begin when class begins. I'm not afraid of him."

"You know for sure?" I ask Ginny as I move into a second-position *plié*.

"I saw him leaving the fourth-level class. He looks real serious and he's carrying his notebook."

A shiver goes through my tired body. The notebook! Saki's notebook is filled with his personal notations and evaluations on each of his dancers — from the youngest to the most *prima* of the *prima ballerinas*. He even keeps an up-to-date record of our weight and measurements — like height, the length of our legs, the degree of our foot arch, and so on.

Sam says, "I heard that he keeps predictions on how he thinks a dancer will do in the future. If they'll make it."

"I wish he'd predicted that Beth was going to have trouble with her knee," I say. "Maybe she wouldn't be having an operation."

"I guess he can't predict injuries," Sam says. She doesn't add what we all know, that Beth shouldn't have kept her knee injury a secret for so long.

"But get this," Ginny says. "He even predicts who will be a dancer in the *corps* for her whole career, and who will become a principal dancer."

I watch my reflection as I do another *plié*. I pull my stomach in tighter.

"And," Ginny continues, "they say he's almost always right. It's like he can see into the future. He has a sixth sense about dancers."

Sam says, "I'd like to know what he thinks my chances are before I go and devote the next six years of my life to this place."

"Me, too," I say.

Sam's strong, lean leg slides along the *barre* in front of me. "It wouldn't do us much good to see it," she says. "He writes his notes in Russian."

Sam and I look at one another and have the same thought: If we could only get our hands on that book, we know someone who reads Russian. We smile at each other and mouth the name "Olga."

Our smiles quickly disappear as Saki, his famous black notebook under his arm, strides into the room. Madame Rostov, a measuring tape draped around her neck, is beside him. They're followed by a senior student pushing a doctor's office scale. Everyone groans.

When it's my turn, I step onto the scale and hold my breath. One hundred pounds, four ounces. I've lost one pound, two ounces since September, and I'm half-an-inch taller. Saki notes it in his book.

He runs his hands along my calf. "Good tone," he says.

He asks me if I have any injuries or special

pains. I decide not to tell him about the leg cramp I had last night. Everyone gets cramps. I don't want to seem like a big baby. As his hand slides down my backbone, he says, "And a nice long line on the back." He notes this in his book while Madame Rostov measures the length of my legs. I don't feel like a person anymore. I feel like a racehorse being judged and talked about. It's like my body doesn't even belong to me.

At lunchtime, all of "Ruth's girls" go to Mario's for pizza. We're on Christmas holidays from PCPS, so we don't have to rush through lunch the way we usually do. We order a deluxe pie.

"It's not fair," Ginny says. "Who can control how they're going to grow?"

"Or how the arch of a foot will change," Olga complains. She sticks out her booted foot in a point. "My foot was much better when I was younger," she scolds as she hits it on the leg of the table. "Most disgusting arch. But," she adds with a proud grin, "it's my disgusting arch, not Saki's." She sighs. "Who'd want it, anyway."

"Adrienne was the fattest," Lyrice says. "Did you see how big she's gotten up top? I bet they don't renew her scholarship."

Ginny includes Sam and me in a glance. It's time to talk to Lyrice about her problem.

"Madame Rostov said that Adrienne's weight gain was normal," I say. "Didn't you hear her say that most girls, even dancers, gain weight at the beginning of — you know."

"The beginning of our bodies becoming a woman's body," Olga explains.

No one says anything for a second. We're waiting for Ginny to bring the subject around to Lyrice. Finally she does. "But, Lyrice," she begins. "You're too thin. Even Saki mentioned it."

"No, I'm not," Lyrice answers. "I eat plenty."

"Yes, but then you throw it up," I blurt out.

"And you could really hurt yourself that way," Sam quickly adds.

Ginny jumps in before Lyrice can answer our accusations. "We think you should tell Ruth and maybe Saki, so you can get some help."

"It's really dangerous to do that to yourself," Olga says. "It's not healthy."

"You can't be a good dancer if you make yourself sick like that," I add.

I thought Lyrice would be upset or angry, but instead she looks around at us and says very casually, "I have a nervous stomach, so I throw up once in a while. What's the big deal?" The waiter puts our deluxe pizza in the middle of the table. "Let's just eat our pizza," she says. "It looks fantastic."

Was I wrong about Lyrice? I wonder. We *are*

under a lot of pressure, and some people *do* throw up more easily than others. I sneak a look at Ginny. Does she think I made the whole thing up?

"Get off those things in here," Mario bellows from behind the counter. Ira, Charlie, and Jason are skateboarding over to our table. "Hey," Jason says as he jumps off his board, "look at that pizza. Great timing."

"Talk about reasons to throw up," Lyrice says, "here are three good ones." Then she whispers to me, "If you tell any more lies about me, Kate Conway, I'm going to tell Ruth about all the rules you've been breaking with Jason."

Jason, Charlie, and Ira are now standing over our table. "Listen," Jason says, "we could all share that pizza — equally, you understand — while Mario makes us another one to share. What do you say?"

I nod.

"Why not?" asks Sam.

"Sure," Ginny agrees.

Lyrice slides out of the booth. "Count me out," she says. "I'll get a sandwich at the deli. I wasn't having a good time, even before you guys came along. *Ciao*." She turns and walks away.

"Boy, is she a snob, or what?" Charlie says.

"She was like that last year, too," Jason tells

him. "She never hung out with us mortals."

"Let's dig into this Mario masterpiece," Ira says, ripping off the biggest piece for himself.

When we finish lunch, there's still half an hour before *pointe* class, so we hang out on 68th Street and watch Jason, Charlie, and Ira show off their skateboard moves. "Wanna try?" Jason asks me. "It's easy."

"I already know how," I tell him. "At home I used to ride my little brother's board."

Charlie holds out his big, pro board. "Not a board like this."

"Of course not," I say.

"I know how," Sam says.

"Prove it," Charlie challenges her as he slams his big board onto the sidewalk. Sam gets on and rides the board to the corner. Jason and Ira ride beside her.

As we run to catch up, Olga is clapping and shouting, "Very good, Sam."

Sam gets off the board at the corner. "But I can't do anything fancy," she tells us.

"Watch this," Ira says as he jumps the curb with his board. "I'll teach you how to do it. You put your . . ."

"Don't bother telling me," Sam interrupts. "I'm not going to risk an injury by trying to do skateboarding tricks."

When we've crossed Broadway, Charlie kicks his board in my direction. "Your turn." I stop it with my foot.

"You sure you know how?" Ginny asks.

"Sure," I tell her. "I've done it before. Besides, I've got good balance." Charlie's big board is heavier than Tommy's kiddie board. But I figure that's good, because I'll be more solidly on the ground.

Jason and I stand next to one another at the top of 68th Street. There's a long strip of sidewalk leading toward West End Avenue. Beyond I see the glint of winter sun reflecting off the Hudson River. A few pedestrians are walking up and down the street. "Don't worry about people on the sidewalk," Jason says. "They'll move out of your way."

I'm on the skateboard. It's moving. I'm moving. But the board is faster than my brother's, and the street is steeper than my driveway in Oregon. And there's a woman pushing a shopping cart across my path. I lean to the left to move out of her way. My left foot falls off the board. I try to balance myself on my right leg while I lift my left foot back onto the board. No good. I lose my balance and fall over onto the sidewalk — on top of my left ankle. I think I hear it sprain. I certainly feel it.

They're all around me — the guys, Sam, Olga,

Ginny, and the woman — all talking at once. They look and sound like they're talking to me from the end of a tunnel.

Sam says, "Where does it hurt? Your leg? What?"

"Are you okay?" Jason asks. "I thought you knew how. I shouldn't have let you."

"That's a very dangerous thing to be doing in the middle of the city," the woman scolds. "You nearly knocked me over, too."

"Oh, no," Olga moans, "poor Kate."

Everything is back in focus. "It's my ankle," I say through tears of pain. I put out a hand to Olga. "Help me up."

While my housemates take classes, I spend the afternoon on the couch with my leg up, my ankle wrapped in an ice pack.

I can hear Ruth in the kitchen scolding Jason. "If I've told you once, I've told you a hundred times, Jason Danner, not to let my dancers use that foolish thing."

"It wasn't his idea," I yell toward them. "Really, Mrs. Danner, it's not Jason's fault. It was all my fault. It was a stupid thing to do."

Ruth comes over to the couch. Jason's behind her. "You're right," she says. "It was stupid. And I blame both of you. You're one lucky dancer. That little sprain will heal quickly."

"I'll miss five performances of *The Nutcracker*," I remind her. "Everyone else in the house is dancing while I'm just sitting here." I blame myself, but I also feel sorry for myself.

"Missing a few performances of *The Nutcracker* is nothing," she says. "The important thing is that you've learned a lesson from this foolishness. Have you?"

I nod.

"And what is it? What's the lesson you've learned?"

"Before doing anything, think about how it will affect me as a dancer."

"That's right. You have potential, Kate. Don't let me down. Don't let yourself down."

After she's gone, Jason sits on the floor next to the couch. "I'm really sorry," he says. "I shouldn't have let you use it."

"It's not your fault," I tell him. "I was being a jerk."

"Why'd you say you knew how to skateboard?"

"I do, sort of." I sit up and move the ice pack around so my ankle won't become entirely frozen. "It's like we said last night. All I do is dance and talk about dancing. I wanted to do something normal for a change."

"Well, you did," he says. "It's pretty normal to sprain your ankle skateboarding."

Ruth yells from the kitchen, "Jason, up to your room to do your homework."

"Okay. Okay," he yells back. "Now there's something else that's normal," Jason tells me. "Homework. You can't tell me you miss being a normal student."

I make a joke about it. Like who'd ever miss homework. But when Jason's gone, I realize I do miss having the time to really think about geography and science and math and history. And I miss having time to read just for fun. That's what I'll do, I think, while I'm laid up with my sprained ankle — I'll finish the book I started on the plane coming to New York.

Monday morning, while Sam and Olga are taking turns in the bathroom and getting dressed to go to class, I lie back on my pillow and think about how much fun I'm going to have just lazing around all day, reading my book.

"I'll get you breakfast," Olga tells me as she grabs her dance bag and heads out of the room. "And bring it to your bed."

"Don't bother," I tell her. "I'll go down myself in a little while." I take my novel out of the nightstand drawer and fluff up the pillows. Just as I'm sinking into them, Sam comes in to see how I'm feeling.

"Better," I tell her. "It doesn't hurt anymore, and it's not swollen at all. It's fun to have a day off."

"Did you hear Lyrice last night?" Sam asks. "Using the bathroom?"

I sit up and whisper, "No. Did you?"

"No."

"I guess now that she knows we know, she won't do it up here anymore," I tell her.

"Do you think we're making too big a deal out of it? Even if Lyrice is throwing up a lot, she keeps dancing. She doesn't look sick."

"But that's an awful thing to do to yourself, Sam. I think we have to tell Ruth."

"Let's talk to Ginny about it first," Sam suggests. "Then we can all tell Ruth together."

Sam leaves, and I snuggle back into my pillows and open my book. I haven't read more than a page when Ruth comes in.

"But, of course, you're going to class, Kate," she tells me. "You'll watch the others. It's a good opportunity for you to study technique."

An hour later, I'm sitting on the floor in a corner of Studio Three watching twenty-three dancers and their mirrored images at the *barre*. Madame Rostov counts out beats and the *pliés* begin. I think of the tens of thousands of *pliés* I've done in my life. I started with one class a week when I was six. At eight, I was taking two classes a week. Then when I was ten, I began taking class every day after school. And on Saturdays, I took a two-and-a-half-hour bus ride to and from Portland for my class with Mr. Randolph.

Pliés, tendus, pas de chats, tour jetés, coupés, pas de bourreés. Thousands and thousands of dance steps. By the time I stop being a dancer, I think, I probably will have danced enough steps to circle the world. How many *pas de bourreés* and *pas de chats* would it take to go around the equator? And what if I could put all my jumps into one big jump? How high would I jump? As high as the top of the Empire State Building? And if I strung all my leaps together in one big one, could I leap over Central Park?

Madame Rostov is scolding the class. "Give more concentration, please. More energy. This is not ballet school in Utah. You are at the National Ballet School. You are, how do you say it in English? Oh yes, 'the cream of the crop.'" Her voice rises to be heard over the three sharp staccato taps of her cane on the hardwood floor. "You must work. Work. Work."

I think, but we can't *all* stay the cream of the crop. Most of us won't make it. Only one out of every fifty students in the school will end up as professional dancers. And only a few of those will become soloists or principal dancers.

I watch the class moving in unison through the combination. Sam's extension looks forced. Olga is pushing her arch and it shows. Lyrice is wobbling off her balance when Madame Rostov isn't looking. I wonder, am I better than they are? Will I be the one who makes it?

For the first time I ask myself, do I want to be?

Madame interrupts my thoughts with a tap of her cane. "Miss Conway, please stretch the body without using the ankle."

I extend my legs on the floor in front of me and lean over them. As she passes me, Madame Rostov taps the base of my spine with her cane and orders, "Pull straight up before dropping over."

I'm at the end of the stretch, my face between my ankles, when I hear a *thud*. I look up. Lyrice has fallen to the floor in a dead faint.

Nine

☐ "Where's Jason?" Ginny asks as she reaches over his empty place to hand me the salad bowl.

"Basketball practice," Sam answers.

I look at Lyrice's empty place. Ruth has taken a dinner tray upstairs for her. "Let's tell Ruth about Lyrice," I say to the others, "as soon as she comes back."

"Maybe Lyrice is telling her herself," Ginny suggests. "Right this minute."

"I doubt it," Sam comments.

The minute Ruth is back in the dining room, Ginny asks, "How's Lyrice?"

"She'll be fine. She's just overtired. She

probably has a touch of flu," Ruth says. "She says her stomach's been upset for a couple of days." She sighs and looks around at us. "I hope that the rest of you don't get it."

"She throws up a lot," I say. "She uses our bathroom, so I've heard her."

"Me, too," Sam tells her.

"It's not good to make yourself throw up," Olga adds.

Ruth laughs. "You made a mistake with your English, Olga. 'To make' is 'to cause to happen.' Lyrice doesn't 'make' herself throw up. She just throws up."

"But she does make it happen," I say. "We think she makes herself do it to keep thin. You know, the way Saki likes us to be."

"Girl dancers, not women dancers," Olga adds.

"What is going on here?" Ruth asks in an annoyed voice.

I try to explain. "It's just that . . ."

"Please be quiet, Miss Conway," Ruth scolds. She looks around at the others. "All of you. Lyrice has an upset stomach. She's working very hard and is fatigued. She's a gifted dancer and an intelligent young woman. I have no reason to believe she has an eating disorder. In any case, this is not your affair." She looks down at her cold beef stew, "And this is a most unpleasant conversation to be having at the dinner table."

No one says a word. I pick at my stew and try not to think about throwup.

Finally Ruth looks up at us and says, "I do not like gossiping" — she scowls directly at me — "anymore than I like skateboarding."

I look down at my stew. I've lost my appetite.

After dinner, Olga goes upstairs to keep Lyrice company while the rest of us do kitchen cleanup. Fifteen minutes later, Sam puts the broom back in the closet, I make a last clean wipe over the counter, and Ginny turns the knob to start up the dishwasher.

While Ruth is making her inspection, the doorbell rings. "That's Saki," she tells us. "There's a benefit for the company after the ballet, so I'll be back quite late. This is your night off from *The Nutcracker*. I want you all to get right to bed. Everyone in this house is overtired. I don't want anyone else passing out on me. A dancer needs her rest."

As we're leaving the kitchen, Sam says, "Let's go to my room."

The second we're behind the closed door of Sam's room, I say, "Ruth doesn't believe us."

Ginny stretches her lean body over the length of Beth's bed and props her chin up on her elbow. "Maybe you two were wrong about Lyrice."

I sit next to her. "I heard her doing it. Lots of times."

Olga and Sam lie across Sam's bed facing us. Sam says, "Maybe she'll stop now. You know, because we're on to her and because she fainted."

"Anyway," Ginny says, sitting up, "I'm sick of this subject. I'm going downstairs and keep her company. I think that's more helpful than gossiping about her."

When Ginny's gone, I tell Sam, "I know I wasn't wrong."

Sam says, "You did what you thought was right, but now it's over. We were probably making too big a deal out of it."

I don't know what I think about Lyrice anymore.

Ten

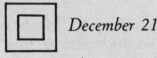 *December 21*

Dear Carole,

I miss you. I miss Oregon. It's especially weird and lonely being so far from home at Christmastime. I was wondering, when I was home did I ever talk about anything but dancing? I've been thinking about all the times after school and on Saturdays when you wanted me to do stuff with you and I couldn't because I had ballet class.

Your best friend,

Kate-who-can't-wait-to-go-home

I put the letter in one of the envelopes that Carole had addressed to herself and lick it closed. It's ten o'clock. Olga's still writing her letter home. "I'm going to sleep," I tell her.

"Good night," she says. "I'm telling my mother what a great person you are. Also that you're a good dancer."

"Olga, you're the one who's great," I tell her.

Just as I reach over to turn off my night-light, Sam and Ginny come in. "Come on. Get up," Ginny whispers.

"Both of you," Sam says as she snatches off my covers. "This is our chance."

"Our chance?" I ask as I pull my covers back up. "For what?"

"Saki's notebook," Ginny answers. "He left his briefcase here while he and Ruth went to that benefit. Hurry."

"The notebook where he writes about dancers?" Olga asks.

"I bet it's in his briefcase," Sam says. "Come on."

"What about Lyrice?" I ask.

"She's sleeping," Ginny answers.

A few minutes later, we're sitting in a row on the couch — Olga in her blue-striped pajamas, Sam in her yellow terry cloth bathrobe, Ginny in her gray satin robe, and me in my leopard pattern flannel pajamas. It's just like a pajama party, except there's no food, no music, no laughing, and no fooling around. We're all perfectly still, staring at Saki's black leather briefcase, which is right where he left it, in the middle of the coffee table.

"Go ahead," Sam finally says to me.

I unzip it and peek in. "You're right, Sam," I whisper. "It's in there." I sit back down between Olga and Sam.

"Who's going to take it out?" Ginny asks.

"You should," I say. "You're the oldest."

"Oh, no," Ginny says. "Not me. I'm too scared."

"I don't care what that dictator says about me," Olga says in a firm voice.

Sam and I look at one another. "Did you tell her?" I ask.

Sam shakes her head. "I thought that *you* did."

"Olga," I explain, "Saki writes his notes about us in Russian. So you're the only one who can read them."

She scowls at us.

"Don't you want to know?" Sam asks her.

Olga shakes her head and asks, "Why do you want to know?"

"I want to know if Saki doesn't think I'm going to make it," Ginny explains to Olga. "Because if he doesn't believe I am, I don't want to keep working so hard. I might as well do

91

something else." She sighs. "Except I don't know what."

Sam kneels in front of the coffee table, takes the notebook out of the briefcase, and holds it out to us. "This book can tell me what he thinks of me."

"He said in class the other day that you're making great progress," Ginny reminds her.

"He must think we can all make it, to give us scholarships," I suggest.

"But we can't all make it to the top," Ginny reminds us. "In this book he says who he thinks has the potential to become a great ballerina."

"It's like this notebook is a crystal ball, and Saki's a fortune-teller," Sam says as she hands it to Ginny.

"A ball like a dance?" Olga asks. "Saki has a special dance party for dancers?"

When I've explained to Olga what a crystal ball is, she says, "I have a crystal ball in my own heart and head. I tell my own fortune. I make myself. Not Mr. Saki-Fortune-Teller."

We all stare at the notebook and think about what Olga said.

Ginny breaks the silence. "I agree with Olga. I don't want to know what he says about me because if I knew, I might not try so hard."

"Even if he says you're going to be great?" I ask her.

"Especially if I'm going to be great. Because if I knew that, then I might not work so hard and in the end, I wouldn't be." Ginny rubs her hand over the soft leather, looks up at us, and grins. "But I'd love to know what he says about you guys." She hands the notebook back to Sam.

Sam takes it, looks at it, then drops it on the coffee table with a thud and jumps up. "No," she says. "I don't want to know, either. So what if he says I'm a no-talent? I'll show him." She's offended, angry, and determined. "No matter what he thinks, I can do it."

"But you don't even know what he's written about you," I say. "Don't you want Olga to read it for you?"

"No," Sam says. "Whatever I do, I do. How can he know how I'll develop? Maybe I'll grow in the way that will give me the best possible ballet body and spirit. It's up to me, not him."

"What about you, Kate?" Ginny asks.

I think for a second. I *do* want to know what Saki thinks of me. Because if I could know for sure I'd be a great ballerina, it might be worth it. All the years of training, of thinking and doing and talking about nothing but dance. But if I won't be great, really great, then maybe it's not worth all this work and dedication. "Yeah," I say as I pick up the book and open it. "I want to know."

93

Olga says, "It's wrong to read another person's private journal. Even Saki's."

"Olga," I explain, "it's not about him, it's about us. It's like a teacher's report card."

"Not exactly," Ginny says, "because the teacher expects you to read the report card. If Saki thought that what he writes would make us better dancers, he'd tell us himself."

Olga folds her arms. "I won't read it."

I look down at the opened page of the notebook and start laughing. "Well, that settles it," I tell them.

"What's so funny?" Sam asks as she comes around the table to look over my shoulder. Sam sees and laughs, too.

"How can you understand to make a joke if it's in Russian?" Olga asks.

"You guys," Ginny says, "what's so funny?"

I turn the book around to show the opened page to Ginny and Olga.

"So it's in English," Olga says. You can read it for yourself."

By now, Ginny, Sam, and I are laughing so hard that tears start rolling down our faces.

"Sure," I tell Olga, "if I want to know when he's going to dinner, or how many dentist appointments he has in January, or when he's teaching the *corps*. This is his appointment book," I explain to her, "for what he does every day.

It's not his dancers' notebook."

Now Olga's laughing, too. That's what we're all doing — reading entries from Saki's appointment book and laughing our heads off — when we see Ruth and Saki walking down the hall toward the living room.

Sam stands, grabs Olga by the hand, and shouts, "This is how you do it, Olga." She yanks Olga around and sings at the top of her lungs, "Boogie, boogie. Boogie, boogie on down."

Ginny stands in front of me and opens her bathrobe and shouts above Sam and Olga's improvised rock-and-roll, "See, pajamas. We're having a pajama party."

I crouch behind the curtain Ginny's made for me with her opened bathrobe and slip Saki's appointment book back into his briefcase.

When I jump out from behind Ginny, I shout, "We're having a party." I do a little boogie step to make it more realistic.

Jason, still half asleep, comes stumbling down the stairs into the room. He wipes sleep from his eyes and asks, "What's going on?" He sees us. "Hey, how come you had a party without inviting me?"

Olga and Sam finally stop dancing and singing. "Oh, hi," Sam says, acting like she's surprised to see Ruth and Saki.

Lyrice has come down the stairs behind Jason.

She takes one look at us and turns around and heads back upstairs.

"Lyrice, are you okay?" Ruth calls to her. "How do you feel?"

Lyrice stops halfway up the stairs and turns to us. "I'm fine," she says. "I'm feeling much better, thank you." She looks around at us, like she's on a stage and we're her audience. "Thank you, all, for being so concerned about me. I really am fine. I've always had a sort of delicate stomach."

Ruth flashes Lyrice a reassuring smile. "I understand, dear. Good night."

"Some of the best dancers have had delicate stomachs," Saki tells Lyrice. "Good night." As Lyrice continues up the stairs, Ruth and Saki turn to the rest of us. "Don't dancers need their rest?" Saki asks Ruth.

"They're upset," she explains.

Saki makes a wide gesture with his arm to include us in our various nightclothes, big smiles on our faces. "This is upset?" he asks. "Very strange."

"They're doing it to hide what's really going on," she explains.

For a panicky moment, Sam and Ginny exchange a look. I see Olga gulp and glance at the briefcase.

"What's really going on?" Saki asks.

"I know what they're trying to hide," Jason says. "They were trying to hide their party from me. I thought you guys — girls — were my friends."

Ruth finally answers Saki's question. "What is really going on is that they're all homesick. It's Christmastime, after all, and they're trying to hide their homesickness by being a little childish."

We can't help it. We start laughing with relief at not getting caught going through Saki's briefcase and reading his appointment book.

Ruth and Saki just stare at us.

Jason starts laughing, too.

Ruth shakes her head in amazement. "This is carrying it too far, girls," she says sternly. "Now up to bed. All of you. You, too, Jason. And don't let me hear a peep."

We do it, but halfway up the first flight of stairs, we hear Saki tell Ruth, "You understand young people very well. That's why you make a perfect housemother for my little dancers." We cover our mouths to hold the laughs back and run the rest of the way upstairs.

We stay awake for another two hours, giggling and whispering about what happened. Finally, after eating every candy bar, cookie, box of raisins, and soda that we've stashed away for an emergency like this, we go to bed.

I'm half asleep when Olga says, "I think this bathrobe party is a good idea."

"Pajama," I mumble into my pillow. "Not bathrobe party. Pajama party." I don't know if Olga can hear me. I don't care because I'm sound asleep.

Eleven

☐ "I've never been so tired in my entire life," Sam tells us as we rush through the crowds on Broadway toward the studio for morning class.

"What about the first week we were here," I remind her.

"Tonight will be hard to dance in *Nutcracker*," Olga says.

"Lucky Lyrice," Ginny comments. "She gets to stay in bed all day." When I think about Lyrice, the "lovely ballerina-who-makes-herself-throw-up-and-lies-about-it," I can't even envy her getting a day off.

I'm amazed at how well we get through class.

Sam does some of her best turns. Ginny's *arabesque* is perfect, and Olga is elegant in her *pirouettes*. During our break between classes, Olga lies down on the dressing room floor, puts her head on her dance bag, and falls asleep in the wink of an eye. I'm about to join her when a voice over the loudspeaker calls out, "Kate Conway to the fitting room, please."

"How come?" Sam asks.

"I gained a couple pounds when I was out with my ankle," I tell her. "My Candy Cane costume is tight."

Everyone in the dressing room, except Olga, is looking at me as I leave. Do the extra pounds show?

I walk down the hall toward the fitting room remembering the desserts I've indulged in, the butter and jam I put on my toast, the candy and cookies in the dressing room, the snacks I ate last night. I think of the extra glass of milk I drank this morning and of how hungry I always feel.

Madame Minoff's cold fingers deftly slip under the costume and pull at a strip of seam around my waist. "There's a little here I can let out," she says. Then she scolds, "Too much cookie and candy."

"I hurt my ankle," I explain. "I was out for five days and couldn't take class."

100

"Oh," she says, "that is different. A dance injury is a serious thing, and sometimes a dancer gains a little weight. So you are a real dancer now if you had a dance injury."

I don't tell her that what I had was a stupid skateboard injury.

Walking down the hall back to our dressing room, I notice that the door of the main rehearsal studio is ajar. I hear Patricia Gordon's voice. I peek in and see her standing in the middle of the studio with Saki. I remember from the day's schedule that she's learning a new role from him for the winter season. She's wearing pale blue leg warmers over a black leotard and tights. Her black hair is tight in a dancer's bun. Glistening sweat drips down the side of her face and beads up along her arms and legs. Hers is a perfect body. All smooth, tight muscles. Not an ounce of fat. The perfect dancer's instrument.

"Again," Saki instructs her. "Higher on the turn and raise into the *arabesque* a split second sooner. Anticipate it."

The piano player begins. She does the dance combination perfectly.

Saki tells her so. "Perfect. I knew you could do it. See — you must listen to me and be a good girl."

I continue down the hall. Good girl? Patricia Gordon is thirty years old. She's a woman. Does

Saki see her as his girl-dancing machine? Does she get measured and weighed like we do? I wonder if she thinks about food all the time, too, and if she stops herself from eating, even when she's hungry.

That night we make magic on the stage for three thousand people. The audience *oohs* and *ahhs* at all the right places. Squirmy children are astonished into wide-eyed, open-mouthed wonder by the growing Christmas tree, life-sized mice, and the battle with the Nutcracker.

The number finished, I place my mouse-head on the rack and stop for a minute to watch the African-American Snowflake make her graceful chocolate-brown spins through the falling snow.

I think of Sam. I know she'll be a ballerina, and become part of the magic and art of ballet night after night. And Ginny, too. She has the talent and determination. I'm not sure about Lyrice. But I do know that after this year, Olga will go on studying in Russia and someday will be back in the United States with the touring company of the Kirov. How proud she'll be to show her Russian friends all that she knows about America. In my mind's eye, the stage with its falling snow has become a crystal ball. A ball that's been shaken to stir up fake snow. Through the snow I see Sam, Ginny, and Olga — perfect ballerinas.

And what about me? I could be a ballerina, too. As I imagine my friends as adult dancers, turning and gliding through the fake snow, I realize that I don't want to be among them. I don't want everything I do as I'm growing up to be about ballet. I feel, deep inside, that I don't want to be a ballet dancer.

"Sam, I'm sorry. I know you're asleep, but I've got to talk to you."

She sits up and switches on the light.

"You're crying!" she exclaims. "What's wrong?"

"I don't want to know my future," I blurt out.

"We gave up the idea of reading Saki's notebook, so don't worry about it." Now she's wide awake. "Oh, no, Kate. Did you find the real notebook? You didn't take it?"

I shake my head. "It's not about Saki or any of that stuff. It's about me. I don't want to study dance anymore. I don't want to devote my whole life to it."

"Oh, Kate, don't give up. You can do it."

"I'm not giving up," I tell her. "I've changed my mind about being a dancer."

"But you love to dance," Sam insists. "You're

just tired and you had that injury."

I go back to my own room and lie in the dark, listing the other people who will think I'm a quitter if I stop dancing. My old dancing teachers — Mrs. O'Brien and Mr. Randolph. I'm their first student to get a scholarship to the National Ballet School. How can I face them if I give it up?

And my parents. They'll be glad that I'm home, but how will they feel about all the time and money they've put into my training? And won't they be embarrassed in front of their friends that I've given up?

I put my little sister on the list. She won't admire me the way she used to. I picture the poster-sized photo of me on *pointe* in my *Coppélia* costume that my mother gave Judy on her fourth birthday. I'm Judy's Patricia Gordon.

My friends at school go on a list all their own. They'll think I'm just saying I don't want to become a dancer as an excuse to cover up that I'm really not good enough. The tears trickle over my earlobes onto the pillow. Maybe I'm not. And if I am, then I am a quitter, which is just as bad.

When we get back from our Christmas Eve performance, Ruth greets us at the door. She's in her best black theater dress, and I think, she's going out, so tonight will be more relaxed. Sam elbows me. She's thinking the same thing, a whole evening in the house — just us — without Ruth. A real pajama party.

"You look nice, Mrs. Danner," Ginny says as we walk into the hall.

"Why, thank you, Ginny." She smiles at each of us. "You'll all look lovely, too, because we're going to a Christmas Eve dinner party. It's a surprise from Saki to the girls in the house. So go right upstairs and put on your very best dresses." She gives Sam a meaningful glance.

"Do I have to wear a jacket?" Jason yells from the top of the stairs.

"It goes without saying, Jason," his mother calls back. "And your leather shoes, not those canvas things."

"It's going to be boring," Jason tells us as we walk past his room. "Too snooty and proper, if you ask me."

"Cheer up, Jason," Ginny tells him. "Maybe the food'll be good."

"Oh, very nice, Samantha," Ruth says when Sam leads our group down the stairs an hour later. Sam's dress is a short white satin sheath with gold lace trim. The rest of us are wearing the same dresses we wore to *The Sleeping Beauty*, with Olga wearing Sam's wild outfit. Ruth's mouth drops open when she sees her in the black miniskirt. "Olga," Ruth tells her, "we are going to a fancy dinner in a proper restaurant, not a discotheque. I would prefer that you dress like the others."

"This is a proper American teenager outfit," Olga says with finality. She shakes her braceleted wrists. "And it's very fancy."

When the cab turns into Central Park, and we see the tens of thousands of little white lights on the trees around Tavern on the Green restaurant, we know where the party is being held.

The eight of us sit at a round table near the Christmas tree. Saki looks handsome in a dark suit with a red tie. Even Jason looks special in a jacket and tie. We order Shirley Temples while Saki and Ruth have champagne.

When our drink order is in front of us, Saki raises his glass. "I'd like to make a toast," he says. We all raise our glasses. "To our scholarship students who are far from home for Christmas." I feel a lump of loneliness in my throat. "Especially," he nods to Olga, "my young Russian dancer who is away from her country." He says something to her in Russian, and they click glasses.

"What did he say?" Sam asks.

Olga has tears in her eyes. "He says he knows how hard it is to be far from my Russian family on the holiday. He was away from Russia for twenty-five years without being able to go home. He says that I am lucky to be able to go home so easily."

But Saki isn't being sad. He's smiling and raising his glass in Ginny's direction. "And to Miss Lee," he says, "who moves up to Intermediate Level Two after the holiday." They clink glasses.

"Thank you," Ginny beams.

"Thank yourself," Saki tells her. "You did it yourself."

"To Lyrice, who dances as light as a feather. You will move up to Intermediate Level Three."

"Thank you," Lyrice says as she raises her glass to meet Saki's. "Thank you for being a wonderful teacher."

Ruth puts down her glass and softly applauds Saki. We all join in. He gestures us to stop. "Enough," he says, "this evening is for you." He turns his smile on Sam and toasts her. "Merry Christmas to Miss Bellows from Boston who sneaks off to jazz class." I gulp. How did he know she was doing that? Does he have spies? "Have you made a choice," he asks Sam, "between Broadway and ballet?"

"Yes," Sam answers. "I've made a choice. I still want to be a ballerina."

"Good. Then instead of jazz class, take extra partnering classes with Madame Lowell starting after the holiday."

We're astonished. Madame Lowell's class is the intermediate-level partnering class. Sam will be the youngest in the class, with the most advanced boys to partner her. Her hand is shaking so much with the excitement of Saki's announcement that when his glass clinks against hers, she spills half her drink into the holly-and-roses arrangement in the center of our table.

Saki turns to me. "To Miss Conway of Oregon. No more injuries with American sports equipment, please."

I raise my glass, ready to clink with him. But he's not finished speaking. "Also, after the holiday, you will move to Intermediate Level Two."

We clink glasses. Everyone says "how fabulous" and "wonderful" and congratulates me.

I try to make my smile look real.

Ruth taps her glass to get our attention. "Congratulations," she says, "all of you." She raises her glass. "Merry Christmas."

Jason yawns when he sees me looking at him. I guess for him, this dinner is boring.

Sam and I go together to the ladies' room between dinner and dessert. "I told you," she says excitedly. "I told you that you were doing great. In the middle of the year, Saki's moving you up. I told you not to give up."

I don't answer.

She's talking to my reflection in the mirror where we both study our mirrored images and fix our hair. "What's wrong with you, Kate? Aren't you excited? Level Two. That's amazing."

"Sam," I tell her, "I don't care what level I'm at. I mean when Saki said that, I didn't even care. I've made up my mind not to come back after vacation. I'm giving up my scholarship."

Sam's hand freezes in midair. "Giving it up? When you're so good? Why?"

"I tried to tell you the other night. I want to have time to do a lot of different things in my life. I'm sick of sacrificing everything for dance." The words are coming out of me in an angry rush. "I don't want to always have to worry about my body — whether it's thin enough or strong enough. . . ." Our eyes meet in our mirrored images. "And I'm sick of looking in the mirror all the time."

Sam's happy expression has dropped into a sad frown.

"I guess you're disappointed in me," I say in a quieter, calmer voice.

Tears have collected in her eyes and leak down her cheeks. "Oh, Kate," she says, "I'm not disappointed in you. I'm crying because I'm going to miss you."

We hug. I'm going to miss Sam, too.

Twelve

"We're not even going to wish you Merry Christmas," my mother tells me on the phone the next morning, "because it won't be Christmas for us until you're home."

"How come we opened our presents then?" Tommy asks.

"Christmas is more than presents," my father tells him.

"When are you coming home?" Judy asks.

"Soon, honey. You just count six days, and I'll be there."

"Will you stay for a long time or a little time?"

Here's my chance, I think. I could tell them

right now that I'll be home for a very long time, that I don't want to come back to New York City and the National Ballet School after vacation. Before I get it out, my father is saying, "Kate's coming home for a nice long visit, Judy. But then she's going back to New York to be a dancer."

"We're all so proud of you, Katie," my mother says for about the three-thousandth time.

I decide to wait until I get home to give them the bad news.

I don't tell Ruth that I won't be coming back until the day before my flight home. We're alone in the kitchen. Everyone else has gone upstairs to pack for the holiday.

"Kate Conway," she says. "I really don't believe this. Come here and sit with me, and we'll get to the bottom of it."

I sit across from her at the small table in the corner. "Would you like a cup of tea, dear?"

I shake my head no. I plant my feet firmly on the floor and square my shoulders against the back of the chair. No one is going to change my mind.

"Now," Ruth begins, "I could understand if you had a body that wasn't growing right for a dancer. Or if you were prone to injury like Beth. Or if you didn't have the talent like — well, like some girls. But it's all working out so beautifully for you. So what is it? What's this nonsense about giving up?"

"I'm not giving up," I tell her. "I've just made a choice not to go on."

"It's not a choice. If you have the talent and you don't develop the gift, you're giving up."

We go back and forth, arguing like this until finally she leans over and takes my hand in hers and says softly, "Kate, I'm just trying to keep you from making the same mistake I made. I could have been a great ballerina — a principal dancer with the National Ballet — and I gave it up because I thought I wanted to live a normal life. A normal life is boring, my dear. Don't give in to the temptation to be ordinary."

"I don't know what a normal life is," I tell her. "But whatever I do with my life will be special for me. I don't want to spend so much time at one thing when I'm still a kid." I let go of her hand. "How can anyone be sure they'll be a great ballerina? I can get an injury anytime, or my knee could wear out like Beth's. Or other dancers will come along who are better than I am and beat me for parts. And, then, when I'm still sort of young, I'll be too old to be a ballerina."

"Everyone takes chances in life," Ruth says. "And for a dancer, the rewards of being on the stage make it worth it."

"Not for me," I say as I stand up. I don't leave the kitchen yet because I have one more thing I want to tell Ruth. Before I lose my courage, I blurt out, "You should think about Jason's feelings when you talk about wishing you'd stayed a dancer. You make him feel like you wish he was never born."

"How dare you speak that way to me, young lady. You seem to be having a lot of trouble minding your own business these days. I suggest you take as much care with your own life as you're taking with other people's."

"I'm sorry if I was rude," I say. "I didn't mean to be."

I leave her sitting there. I hope that she's thinking about what I said about Jason and not just being angry at me.

When I come into our bedroom, Olga looks up from her packing. "Did you tell Ruth?" she asks me. "Did she change your mind? Will you stay?"

"Olga, no. I didn't change my mind." Olga sits next to her suitcase on the edge of the bed. Tears leak out the corners of her eyes.

I put my arm around her. "Don't cry."

"I cry," she tells me, "because I am going to miss you. But I also cry because I miss my family. I understand why you want to go home. I left home in Kiev to study dance at the ballet school

114

in Moscow when I was eight years old. Sometimes it's very lonely not to be with my family."

"You're going to be with Sam's family for two weeks, Olga. That'll be fun."

Sam comes up behind me and places her hand on my shoulder. "You're going to love my folks," Sam tells Olga. "And my friends are neat." Then she says to me, "I wish you were coming to Boston with us."

"That would be great," Olga adds. "I wish that, too."

I sigh. "Well, I guess I'll go down and tell Jason."

I'm about to knock on the door of Jason's "Private Property — Beware of Guard Dog" room when I stop my fist in midair. Someone is already there. I lean closer and hear Ruth's voice. I don't knock and I don't stay to listen to what she's saying. As I quietly climb the stairs back to my own room, I hope that Ruth can make Jason believe she loves him better than ballet. More than that, I hope that she really does, because Jason Danner is no fool. He can tell a phony, even when it's his own mother.

The next morning Jason appears in our doorway to tell us, "My mother said I should help you weaklings with your suitcases."

"Weaklings?" Sam shouts. "Put 'em up, Jason Danner."

115

She beats him at arm wrestling — with both the right and left arms. Then she and Olga carry their own suitcases downstairs.

I point to my two big bags. "I could use some help, Jason."

"You're taking all that stuff for just two weeks? Remind me never to go on a trip with you."

I finally say it. "I'm going home for good, Jason."

He's shocked. "How come? You're like the best one in your class. I don't get it. Did they kick you out because of the skateboarding business?" His face flushes with anger. "That's not fair. I'll talk to my mother, to Saki, I . . ."

"No, no, Jason. No one kicked me out. I decided myself. I'm sick of ballet. I want to just be a normal kid. Like you."

"Maybe you could not take as many classes for a while and still live here."

"That wouldn't work, Jason. Not with the NBS. You know that. It's all or nothing with them."

He looks down at his feet and practically whispers, "You're my favorite one. I don't want you to leave."

"I'll miss you, too, Jason," I say.

"If you're going to be a normal girl now, I wish you'd do it in New York City. I could teach you how to really skateboard." He looks me straight in the eye and for an instant, I can see how sad I've made him. "Charlie and Ira aren't going to stand for this," he threatens. "We might kidnap you."

I start laughing. "My friends in Oregon would like you, too, Jason," I tell him.

"I'll write to you if you'll write to me," he says.

"Deal," I answer.

At breakfast, Ruth gets our attention by tapping a spoon on her juice glass. "Girls, I know some of you have been homesick. But I guarantee that after a vacation from dance and some time at home with your friends and family, you will *all* be very happy to be back to dancing and your life as a dancer." She nods to Lyrice. "Isn't that so, Lyrice?"

"It was for me," Lyrice tells us. "When I got home last January I was so happy to be there, I thought, what if I don't want to leave home again at the end of vacation? But after a few days at home, my whole body was aching to get back to being a dancer. And I missed my dancer friends here in New York, even more than I missed my friends from home when I was here."

"Kate, I'd like to talk about you," Ruth says. Everyone's eyes turn on me. I slump in my seat. "Now, let's not be shy," she chides. "Everyone knows that you've given up your scholarship. I've thought a great deal about our little talk last night, and I've decided to give you a second chance."

I sit up tall and practically shout, "But I don't want a second chance."

"Just listen, please. You have a serious case of homesickness. Oregon and New York are a whole country apart. I'm sure life in Eugene, Oregon, is quite different from life in New York City. Just as I am sure that life with your little family is different from our life here at the brownstone."

"But —"

She raises her hand to stop my words. "Just let me finish. I haven't told Saki about your decision to give up your scholarship. You and I will talk by phone after you've been home for a few days. Meanwhile, discuss all this with your parents. Think it through a little longer."

"I have been thinking it through," I tell her.

"Kate," Sam says, "Mrs. Danner's right. Talk to your mother and father."

"Maybe I won't lose my favorite roommate," Olga comments.

"Try it, Kate," Ginny suggests. "What have you got to lose?"

Lyrice doesn't say anything, but Jason shouts, "Why not? Go for it."

"But I've already made up my mind," I protest.

"Don't you see," Ruth says. "I'm giving you another chance. Take it. Why, if I'd had a second chance . . ." She stops in midsentence and doesn't tell us again how her life was ruined when she got pregnant with Jason. Instead, she gets up and tells us, "I'm making more toast for you girls. I don't want you traveling on empty stomachs." As she passes Jason, she leans over and kisses him on the top of his curly head and gives him a little hug. It's the first time I've seen her kiss and hug Jason. He blushes.

The pilot tells us over the loudspeaker system, "Those of you seated on the right side of the plane have a good view of the Grand Canyon." I look through the window. What I see takes my breath away. It's like the photograph in my sixth-grade geography book, only bigger and better. The blue sky above the canyon seems to go on forever. The striped purple-, pink- and earth-colored walls of the canyon rise in sharp angles above the curving river of blue-gray water that snakes its way through the chasm. The Grand Canyon. I wonder, will I ever go on a raft down that river? I can't know the future, but if I want to do it, I bet I will. I wonder if I would even have had the idea of going rafting in the Grand Canyon if I were still going to be a dancer.

I feel happy not knowing what I'll be interested in, what I'll study, and what I'll learn when I'm back in regular school. I love that by not being in the dance studio every day, I'll have hours freed up to do other things. I'm relieved that I won't have to worry so much about what I eat or whether I'll injure myself.

Then I remember how much I'll miss my new friends from the bunstone — especially Sam and Olga. I hope we'll be pen pals, but I wonder if they'll find time to write back to me when they're so busy being dancers. Maybe someday, I think, I'll want something as badly as they want to become dancers. Maybe someday there will be something I'm willing to sacrifice everything else for. But not now. Not when I'm thirteen years old.

I finally see what I've been looking for on the river — the speck of a raft. That's how I want my life to be, I think, like a raft going down a magnificent waterway, with new experiences around every turn in the river.

The elderly man sitting next to me leans over to look at the view and says, "Mighty beautiful, isn't it?"

"I've never seen it before," I tell him.

"You going home or going to visit someone?" he asks me.

"I'm going home," I tell him. "I live in Eugene, Oregon."

"Going home," he says. "There's no place like home."

"That's right," I tell him. But at the mention of home, I feel my stomach turn over.

"Home is where the heart is," he tells me.

Yes, I think, but home is also where my parents are. My parents who don't know I've changed my mind about becoming a dancer. I decide to tell them about Beth's knee and Lyrice's eating disorder, about Patricia Gordon's bloody toe shoe, about my being weighed and measured like a racehorse, about my body aching from the strain of dance classes, and how awful it is to worry about every little thing you eat. I figure they'll understand those reasons better than my wanting my life to be like a raft in a river.

Thirteen

Judy is the first one to reach me when I walk through the gate into the airport lobby in Eugene. She jumps all over me with hugs and kisses as she yells over and over, "You're here. You're here." I hug and kiss her back.

"Big deal," Tommy says.

I untangle myself from Judy's hugs and go over to him. "Hey, there, Tommy," I say. "I missed you, too." I put my arm around his shoulder and plant a big kiss on his cheek.

He blushes and shrugs just like Jason did when Ruth kissed him.

Mom and Dad are full of hugs and kisses, too.

"Will you open your presents as soon as we get home? Please?" Judy says when we're all in the car and on our way home.

"Sure," I tell her. "As soon as I put my stuff in my room."

As I take the first step into my own room, I start to cry. So it's through tears that I see my old pine bunk bed, my worn plaid carpet, my bureau with its attached mirror, my white Formica desk, the books and old stuffed animals on my bookshelves. I love this room. I want to cuddle up under my quilt knowing all my stuff is back in my drawers and closet and that I won't have to leave again in two weeks.

My mother and father, each carrying one of my suitcases, come into the room behind me. I stay facing the wall so they won't see the tears that I can't stop. But my mother sees my reflection in the mirror. "My goodness, Kate," she says. "What is it? What's wrong?"

"I'm so happy to be home," I tell her.

"Those aren't tears of happiness," my father says. "Tell us what's wrong."

"Nothing's wrong. It's just that I'm glad to be home. I love my room," I tell them. "I want to . . ." I swallow the words instead of saying them.

My mother says, "Come here and sit on the bed with me."

My father sits on the edge of my desk. My mother and I sit on my bottom bunk and she says, "Now, tell us what's upsetting you so. I know something is wrong, Kate."

"I want — I want to wake up every morning in this room."

"Why, Kate," my mother says, "there's no reason to cry now. You're home. You'll have a nice vacation and see all your friends."

"Sounds to me like you've had a pretty serious case of homesickness," my father says. "You'll probably feel differently after you've been home for a few days."

"I don't want to go back to New York."

My father's alarmed. "What happened there?" he asks. "Was the work too hard? Did they mistreat you?"

"Everyone was nice to me. And I was promoted to the next level."

"Promoted?" my mother says. "Already? Why, usually the promotions at the National Ballet School are in June. That's wonderful, Kate. It's the best ballet school in the country, and you were promoted after only four months."

"I don't want to do ballet anymore."

"But you love ballet," she insists. "You spent

your whole childhood in ballet slippers. Remember how you wanted to go to extra dance classes when your friends were playing?"

"That was then. Now I've changed my mind. I want dance to be just *part* of my life," I tell them, "not my whole life. I want to go to school on the school bus like a regular kid. I want to have time to read books and learn more about math and science. I want to learn to speak another language, and maybe learn to draw like Carole. And on weekends, instead of going to dance classes, I want to spend time with my friends and learn to skateboard and maybe play tennis." I look at them and say with all the determination I feel, "I don't want to be a ballet dancer."

"Well, then," my father says softly, "it's your decision, Kate."

"If ballet isn't what you want, Katie," my mother says, "then, of course, you shouldn't be doing it."

I look up at them. "But all the money you've spent on me. And everyone thinks I'm like this big deal. You'll be embarrassed if I stop. You must be disappointed in me."

"Katie," my father says, "you're just a kid. You shouldn't be spending all your time at one thing unless you want it very badly."

"Oh, my goodness," my mother exclaims, her

face in a big glowing smile. "This means you'll be staying home and not going back to New York."

"That's what it means," my father says.

My mother pulls me into a squeeze.

My dad comes over and pats me on the head. "Welcome home, Kate," he says. "I missed you."

Judy yells from the bottom of the stairs, "Can we have presents, please."

"Come on," Tommy shouts, "you promised."

I squirm out of my mother's hug and go to my door to yell back to my brother and sister, "I'm coming, you guys. I just have to get your presents out of my suitcase."

At two o'clock in the afternoon on New Year's Eve, we're gathered around the Christmas tree. Tommy and Judy sit under the tree. I sit on the couch with my mom. My dad plops into the easy chair.

The little colored lights on the tree are lit, and there are at least two dozen candy canes hanging from the boughs. But the rest of the decorations are homemade. Some are ancient, like the animal crackers that I painted in nursery school. From fourth grade there are bright pieces of felt that we'd cut into shapes of stars, bells, and Christmas trees, then trimmed with glue and sparkles. Last year, in seventh grade, they'd taught us how to do origami, and I made a dozen folded paper animal decorations with silver and gold paper. And now there are decorations that Tommy and Judy had made.

"I put 553 cranberries on that string," Tommy proudly informs me. "And I only pricked myself with the needle once." I picture Patricia Gordon in *The Sleeping Beauty* swooning into her hundred-year sleep from a needle prick.

Judy hands me a gift. "Open mine first," she says. "Please."

Judy's present is a small white comb-and-brush set and a dozen covered rubber bands. "For your dance bag," she explains.

"Or your school bag," my mother comments.

"But I got it for her dance bag," Judy emphatically declares. My mother and I exchange a glance. I decide to wait until after presents to tell Judy and Tommy that I'm not going back to New York City.

I know Judy loves the yellow sweater with a fuzzy pink cat on it that I give her because she puts it on right away.

Tommy's gift to me is a see-through plastic case filled with the little useful things a dancer needs every day. There's a tube of liniment for sore muscles, packs of Band-Aids for blisters, cotton balls, and lamb's wool for my toe shoes. Plus a sewing kit with needles and two spindles of pink thread — for sewing the elastic on my ballet slippers and the ribbons on my toe shoes. There's even a pair of scissors in their own little leather holder. "I didn't get it myself," Tommy tells me. "Mom did it."

"Well," my father says, "those are useful items for any person to have, whether they're a dancer or not."

Tommy unwraps the gift I've brought him. It's a brightly colored, glossy poster of a skateboarder at the height of a flip. "I never saw that one before," he says, which means that he loves it. I tell him that I know just what skateboard he should move up to in the spring, and that I'll contribute the first twenty dollars to his getting one.

"Where'd you get the money to buy all this stuff?" he asks me. He turns to my mother. "Did you give it to her?"

"I got paid for dancing in *The Nutcracker*," I tell him.

"You got a job!" he exclaims.

For the first time in his life, I've done something that impresses Tommy. I wonder how he'll feel when he finds out I'm not going to do it anymore.

Next I open the present from my mom. "I made them myself," she says as I unfold pale blue handknit leg warmers. "You can wear them for outdoor sports."

"I thought you didn't know how to knit, Mom."

"I learned so I could make those for you," she tells me proudly. She reaches into the new knitting basket next to the couch and pulls out a photo she's clipped from *Dance Magazine*. "I took this picture to the yarn shop and said, 'I want to knit leg warmers just like these for my daughter.' When I said your name, they recognized it from the article about you in the Eugene *Clarion*." She looks embarrassed. "Anyway, they taught me how."

I take the picture she holds out. It's of Patricia Gordon in her pale blue leg warmers. "You did great, Mom," I tell her. "Thank you."

She says the lily of the valley foaming bubble bath and powder I give her is "just perfect."

When I hand my dad his present, I tell him, "You're always saying how hard it is to juggle everything you have to do. I thought these might help." The present is a book about juggling, with red, white, and blue juggling beanbags.

Tommy and Judy toss the beanbags back and forth while I open the present from my father. It's the biggest present of all — a huge pictorial book on the history of the National Ballet Theater. "40 photos in full color, 300 in black and white," the cover announces. It's the same book that Beth, Sam, Olga, and I looked at in the ballet bookstore the first day of ballet classes in New York. I know how expensive it is. I've never had a book that costs so much money.

"You can take it back and get store credit," my father says. "But maybe you'd like to have it as a memento of your dance period."

"It's beautiful, Dad," I tell him as I flip through the first section. I stop at a picture from the early days of the company. It's of a younger Saki standing near a dancer who's poised at the *barre,* ready to begin a *plié.* He's tapping her on the stomach with his cane. "I can hear what Saki's saying," I tell my family. I try to imitate his Russian accent when I repeat his, "Tuck, Tuck. Please — the posture, the stomach."

I look at the dancer on the facing page — a beautiful woman on *pointe* whipping through a turn in a swirl of lacy pink silk. She looks familiar. Just as I've recognized the face, I read the caption: "Ruth Cranston in the premiere of the stunning ballet Saki created for her — *Evening Variations.*" It's our Ruth. I remember how Sam and I had looked for Ruth's name in the index of this book. We'd looked under "Danner." Now I realize that's why we couldn't find it. Ruth's last name was Cranston when she was a dancer. Danner must be her married name.

I flip forward through the book. There's

another picture of Ruth in a principal role. And then no more. Ruth was right, after all. She was a great dancer before she had Jason.

"You going to read the whole book right now?" my father asks.

I look up at him. "Sorry," I say.

"Poor Kate," my mother says. "All your presents are about the ballet."

"Yeah. But that's okay. I can use them for other things."

"She still has hair to comb," my father says.

"And legs to keep warm," I add.

"The leg warmers will be good for cross-country skiing in the mountains this winter," my mother says.

Judy has draped my leg warmers around her neck and is dancing around the room. "But these are dancing leg warmers," she says. "Not skiing leg warmers."

"Are you going to make some more money when you go back?" Tommy asks.

"I'm not going back," I tell him.

"Kate is coming home to stay," my father says.

"Well, at least until I finish high school," I explain. "I'm not going back to New York City, Tommy, because I've decided not to be a ballet dancer."

Judy jumps on my lap. "Goodie, goodie," she

yells. "Does that mean you'll play with me?"

"Sure," I tell her.

"Will you teach me how to use my new skateboard when I get it?" Tommy asks.

"Sure. As soon as I learn how to do it myself."

The phone rings. "I bet that's for you," my mother says.

I answer it. It is for me. It's Carole. "Carole," I tell her. "Come on over. Can you come right away?"

"I have a Christmas present for you," she says.

"Does the present you got me have anything to do with the ballet?"

"No," Carole says. "I thought you might be a little sick of ballet. So I got you . . ." She stops herself midsentence and laughs. "Very tricky, Kate Conway. Trying to get me to tell you what I got you. Hey, you're not disappointed that it doesn't have to do with the ballet, are you?"

"No," I tell her. "I'm really glad. Come quick. I can't wait to see you."

A few minutes later, I'm alone in my room. I open my suitcase and dig through piles of sweaters, jeans, underwear, and dance gear and pull out the plastic bag of Nutcracker snow that I'd scooped off the stage as a souvenir. I take it downstairs. Dancing on stage in *The Nutcracker*. It's like a dream now. A dream of being in a fairy tale, in a life of make-believe. I sprinkle the shiny fake snow on the dark green boughs of our live Christmas tree. While I'm doing it, I look through the living room picture window and see that snow is falling outside.

"It's snowing," I yell. "It's snowing real snow."

"That's the kind it usually snows," my father calls from the kitchen. "What'd you expect — soap flakes? I'm just glad your plane landed before this started."

"It's snowing! It's snowing!" Judy shouts as she comes running into the living room. "Look."

"I see."

"Can we go play in it?"

"Okay," I tell her. "Let's go."

We put on our coats and rush out into the backyard. The flakes are big and soft, just like the ones in *The Nutcracker*. We stick out our tongues to taste the cold and wet of them. These snowflakes are real.

About the Author

Jeanne Betancourt, the author of over a dozen books, makes her Scholastic Hardcover debut with *Kate's Turn*. Her other books include two Scholastic Point titles — *The Edge* and *Between Us,* an ALA Book for Reluctant Young Adult Readers — as well as Children's Choice Award winners *Sweet Sixteen and Never . . . , Not Just Party Girls,* and *More Than Meets the Eye.* Her novel for middle readers, *The Rainbow Kid,* was followed by four more Aviva Granger stories: *Turtle Time, Puppy Love, Crazy Christmas,* and *Valentine Blues,* also a Children's Choice Award winner. Betancourt's original teleplays for ABC After School Specials have received numerous awards, including six Emmy Award nominations, two Humanitas citations, and the National Psychological Award for Excellence in the Media. The author taught for seventeen years before becoming a full-time writer. She lives in New York City and rural Connecticut.